First Edition Paperback

ISBN: 978-0-6456898-4-6

UNDER A SUMMER SKY IN JANUARY

NEPTUNE HENRIKSEN

Content Notes

- Coarse language from the onset and throughout

- Major story themes of cheating, emotional betrayal, and emotional immaturity

- Character themes of strained, and emotionally-abusive, relationships between queer teenagers and parents. Including: emotional neglect, controlling parenting, distant and dismissive parenting, and queer erasure by parents

- Use of reclaimed queer language, by queer characters

- One depiction of queer slurs used by a parent towards their child

- One depiction of fatphobic language used by a parent towards their child

- Brief allusions to a hyper-"clean" attitude towards food, from parent to teenager (one mention, general themes of underlying parental control of teenager's eating behaviour and habits)

- One visceral and emotional description, and depiction, of food. This is used as a metaphor for sexual desire

- Brief allusions to the spiritual and divine

- Brief allusions to illicit substances, both as metaphor, and as past use (no depiction)

- Themes of not practicing one's religion (Islam) and straying from one's culture (Egyptian)

- Themes of small-town queer loneliness and isolation. Depicted with era-specific communication technology and resources of 2010, 2011, and 2012. With 2011 being the story's main setting.

- Multiple mentions of, and allusions to, teenage sexual desire, masturbation, and urge to have sex for the first time

- One passing mention of a mother's experience growing up in Zimbabwe (circa 1960's – 1980's), and concern for her sexual safety in that context

- One explicit sex scene

Also: This story DOES NOT employ the 'Bury Your Gays' trope.

12:00am 31st January 2011

There Is,

And Always Will Be,

A Before And After

Oh, that powerful vibrant sky, watercolours of lush tangerine, staining and bleeding into calmest lavender, seeping into scattering clouds, tinging turquoise and rose upon their soft whites.

A dream, a vivid memory, bright and inescapable, born from the scorching day, stretching and winding into a long-awaited sunset, bringing the calm, closing the day, dissolving the heat into hazed imagining. Wiping the slate clean for another short night.

The quietest respite at the conclusion of the pulling January.

How the days melt together, and yet, linger like an unwelcome guest. Unbroken by the routine of school and homework, unwatched by parents and teachers, creating a pause that holds the summer in its teeth, daring us to come closer, and take the sun from its grin.

Burns and shade and lungs ravaged. Baking under the azure canvas, scurrying inside to try and avoid the heat, driving with windows down and the air rushing in, like fools falling in love, it can't be helped.

Ushering in hurt and pleasure, treasured moments and regretful missteps, tearful truths and electric dances, all while the sky tells one story, and the clock tells another.

But of course, wanting and being are two different things, and in the brightest, harshest light of summer, there's nowhere to hide.

With nights so short and days so long, there's little room for secrets.

7:13pm 17th January 2011

FUCK YOU RIGHT THROUGH

THE BELLY BUTTON

I HOPE YOU GET FUCKING SEPSIS

"Why did you do it?" August asks, her voice unsteady, every muscle in her body working hard to force the words out. "What were you thinking? Did you think... I mean, d-did you think about how it would... hurt me?"

Celeste cowers under the weight of August's words, cutting right to their bones, and they're unable to look August in the eye. The guilt knotting deep and low in their belly, eating from the inside out.

"Yes." Celeste replies, arms crossing, body folding, cerulean eyes low.

A beat. quiet and violent. Anger rising.

August can feel the white-hot malice rushing through her veins. Boiling and painful. Undampened by the pouring rain, beating down on the awning above.

"Is... is that all you have to say?" August asks, fists clenching, bistre eyes shooting to the sky, hoping to hold the tears in.

"I don't think there's anything... I-I can say..." Celeste tries, flashing a look to a tense August, seeing the effect of her words, scrambling to find ones that could fit. "A-anything that can r-really get across how... how s-sorry I am, and... h-how wrong I was."

August can feel the urge to scream, to cry, to slap Celeste right across their cheating face, all fighting to come to the surface, to express this burning betrayal.

"You could start by..." August forces out, jaw tight, full lips still, breath fast and scalding. "By saying that you were wrong... and even... that you're sorry."

Celeste looks again to August, catching the words as each one escapes, shame rushing her system, sweaty and sticky, even as the heat-breaking rain pelts hard around them.

"You're... you're r-right." Celeste concedes, eyes looking through mousy blonde locks, words full of penance. "I was wr-wrong. Really re-really wrong and I'm... so fucking s-sorry, I'm so sorry August."

Their words hit August where she was already bleeding. Why not call her: 'August Tandi-Andersen, child of Dr. Faye Tandi and Mx. Alf Andersen', while they're at it.

Though perhaps a nickname, or term of endearment, would plunge the knife in further, cut through the fleshy insides, spilling fiery burgundy onto the handle, and down onto the concrete.

"And I th-think like, why I'm so like, q-quiet..." Celeste begins again, seeing the hurt her words are causing, but knowing she has to push on. "I th-think... I'm quiet b-because... because... my brain is, like, tr-trying to say all this st-stuff and I want it to c-come out... right."

August nods. Small and pulsing with anger. Breaths weighty, puffing out her chest completely, the air granting her strength and patience with each inhale.

Small sprinkles sinking into her pumpkin t-shirt, sticking to brown skin, gluing short, dark, ringlet curls to her tense jaw, the water inescapable, finding its way onto August, like the rage. Twisting and winding and seeping through her body, despite her best efforts to remain as calm and open as possible.

"Because I-I think... well, m-maybe I know... that t-there's nothing, not one th-thing, like, at all, that I can say to t-take any of it b-back." They continue, watching August inflate and deflate, cursing their past choices. "I d-don't... like, I don't th-think there's anything I can s-say that can r-really fix any... any of th-this."

August breathing Celeste's words in, bobbing on the balls of her feet, gaze locked on the awning, unaware of watching cerulean eyes.

"Ok, I mean... that's a good start." She replies finally, words tight, as though they can barely get past her rose lips.

"And I mean... If it's any c-consolation..." Celeste continues, unsure if she's digging her own grave, or stepping into the cleansing light of forgiveness. "It was only th-the... one time."

"I don't know if it is, Cee." August stiffly replies, jaw tight enough to crack walnuts, rich rage raspberry bubbling under prominent brown cheeks. "But like, I think on some level I... did wanna know."

"Well, I'm g-glad to… help with th-that at least." Celeste manages, the tiniest bit of humour in their tone.

August snaps her focus to Celeste, bistre eyes potent enough to cut right through human bone.

"You're making jokes right now." She accuses, tone stern and bold, pure venom running through her words. "Are you fucking serious?"

"Sorry, I… th-that was fucked up. I didn't- I mean… th-that was stupid." Celeste apologises, feeling pure regret run right through her.

All at once, the voices are swirling, as they often do. Affirming that they're not worthy of love, of tenderness, not by August, not by anyone.

And, if they've poisoned the well with August, they've not just lost a girlfriend, but a best friend too.

Only an Absolute Fuckup could fuck up so royally.

"Yeah." August agrees, looking Celeste dead in the eyes, ablaze with anger. "You did fuck up. It was stupid."

So simple, so genuine, searing through right to the core.

"…yeah." Celeste admits defeat, small and recoiling.

The voices. Spitting their venom. Correct and gloating. Circling, sinking, like the rain, soaking deep into Celeste, finding the smallest spaces, and growing riddling roots, right into the soft flesh.

"Ok, well…" August replies, rage subsiding, coming back into her body, finally feeling the ricocheting rain sink into light Summer clothes.

"You probably wanna break up, right?" Celeste asks, returning her gaze to August.

She stares back. Dark eyes usually shining richest honey, now burning like devastating fire.

"What are you talking about right now?" August questions, disappointment flying through her words, like bullets through glass. "What are you even...?"

"Like, do you w-wanna... break up, or like... t-try and work through this?" Celeste prods, brave enough to be honest, now at least.

August looks up the awning, bowing and buckling under the thunderous water, pelting it with no remorse. Counting to ten, trying to avoid saying something she can't take back.

"Be honest, Cee, do you want to work through this?" She asks, eyes fixed on the rain.

Celeste tries to start their sentence several times. Clumsy half-words flopping out of their mouth, before being pulled back, all the while, unable to look up from dirty, white Converse, face hidden by their fringe.

"Ok. You think about it, and get back to me." August cuts through, looking to Celeste, gaze boring into short mousy hair.

She's waiting. Hoping Celeste will look at her. Wishing upon a star, for this teenager to cross a heart, and hope to die.

But as they feel August's gaze on them, Celeste can't bring themself to look up from their shamefully shuffling shoes.

"I'll go th-"

"I d-don't think..." Celeste tries, hoping this one will come all the way out. "t-that I want to work it... out. I'm s-sorry..."

Molten wrath. Coming up from the cement. Into crème Volleys. Coursing through bare legs. Past lime shorts. Up through the torso. Under a thin pumpkin t-shirt. Settling in the shoulders. Wrapping around the neck.

Eyes closing, breathe in, counting, breathe out.

"Ok." August replies simply.

Heavy silence. Potent and hateful. Neither moving. Seconds stretching into hours. Horrid and permanent. Scarring instantly.

And she's gone. Walking into the pounding rain, soaking into her clothes in seconds, gluing the thin fabric to brown skin, translucent and exposing. But she can't care.

August opens the car door, soaking rain into the seat, shivering, alone and angry.

Deep breath. Loud scream. Cleansing. Exorcising. Scratching on the way out.

Staring forward. Hands on the top of the steering wheel. Forehead sinking to knuckles. Tears coming thick and fast.

It's not okay. And it won't be okay for a while.

8:21pm 17th January 2011

My Parents?

Ignoring Me And My Needs?

It's More Likely

Than You Think!

"Celeste, Darling, is that you?" Lydia calls, hearing the heavy front door close.

"Yeah, mum, it's me!" Celeste calls back, kicking off her soaked Converse, and placing them in the rack.

"Very good, Darling! Dinner in thirty!"

"Ok thanks!"

Celeste standing stony in the entrance, engulfed in the layers of perfumes, colognes, and dirty shoes, staring blankly down the corridor, knowing no one would come to bother them, or welcome them. That delight is reserved for scolding purposes only.

Her mind running away from her, doubting if she ever made a correct choice, at any point along the journey of the last six months.

Unfocused and weary, they trudge wet socks upstairs to their room, each stair carrying weight and questions, needles driving in with every step, painful and deserved.

Of course, her room has been tided and primed by Patricia, while she's been out, and a defeated Celeste lumbers in, closing the door and sinking to the floor, soaked back against the pearl-painted wood.

Scanning the immaculate room, they take in all the little things that made it appear to be theirs, while in fact, being heavily edited and completely curated by their mother.

The photos of her and August, laid out in expensive, champagne frames, not messy and free like in August's room.

The bed perfectly made, with far too many beige display pillows, on top of Egyptian cotton sheets, all neutrals, despite Celeste's many pleas for something brighter, or a bold design with a fun pattern.

No. Their mother insisted on muted colours only. And what Mrs. Lydia Breadseed says, goes.

The closed door to her closet, behind it clothes picked out by her mother, just feminine enough, but not too flashy or bright.

Not like at August's house. She could always keep her closet open, the contents on display most times, even when Celeste would come to visit.

It never felt like August's family was performing for Celeste the way Lydia and Timothy would put on a show for any guest.

A knock at the door breaking into their thoughts.

"Darling! Dinner!" Her mother's voice called. "It's Mexican, Patricia made it! It's filled tortillas baked in sauce and cheese, it smells divine. Don't let it get cold, Darling."

Celeste clears their throat as quietly as they can, wiping away a few tears that had escaped their cerulean eyes, and steadies themself to speak as evenly as possible.

"Thanks, Mum! I'll be there in a minute, just changing out of these wet clothes into my comfies!"

"Lovely, Darling, see you in a mo!"

Celeste doesn't dare move until she can no longer hear her mother's footsteps.

Crawling to their closet, Celeste manages to shakily stand, open the sliding doors, and scan the contents for their comfy clothes, before falling right back down, their knees giving way, and their breathing becoming ragged.

She knows what this is, and she's gotta get it over with, so she can avoid questions about her day over enchiladas.

The panic attack comes fast and painful, Celeste covering their mouth, trying to keep any noise from drifting into the corridor. Tears streaming down their face, as they lay on the carpet in the foetal position, mouthing the words to Mary Had A Little Lamb, their go-to for trying to bring themself back to any present in which they might be needed.

A hard knock on the door.

She's frozen. Dazed and exhausted, hand over her mouth, barely back in the well-kept room.

"Celly, get down to tea *right now*." Her father's voice demands, his tone stern and laced with British social decorum "I know you're changing, but hurry up."

Celeste attempts to reply, but luckily enough, the footsteps fade on their own, Timothy not bothering to wait for a reply. His curtness having one advantage.

They clumsily change on the floor, pulling and pushing as quickly as their fatigued body will allow. Treacherously standing, they do their best to dissipate face puffiness, hoping they can chalk it up to a lie about allergies, or a false adverse make up reaction.

Though, at the table, no one questions her. Instead, mocking her for taking so much time to come to the table, and critiquing her comfy clothes, and the body beneath them.

The words don't hit their ears, they simply half-smile, nodding when needs must, and eating their food in silence.

The same silence holding onto her entire evening.

Showering silently, crawling into bed silently, watching a DVD on their laptop silently, and falling asleep during the final scene in silence.

No one checking in on her, only the two other actors insisting she perform with them. It's a lonely play that no one attends, with last-minute script changes that drill into the nerve.

But maybe, just maybe, if they pretend hard enough, they will be ok.

8:07pm 17th January 2011

Min Papa?

Derhjemme Nu?

It's More Likely

Than You Think!

"Kære!" Alf calls, taking off their dish gloves and walking to greet August as she takes off her shoes. "Hvordan har du?"

"Ikke så godt." August responds, taking her father into a fierce embrace, and holding tight. "Something happened with Celeste."

"Jeg tor det var veldig-"

"Nei." August cuts in, pulling back from the embrace, tears coming to the surface again.

"Come kære, come and we sit."

Alf leads his daughter to the large, faded butterscotch couch, with its many bright patterned cushions, and small warm blankets. A calming, embracing, respite.

The pair sitting down gently, the weight of emotions heavy on both their shoulders, as the post-rain wind blows through the open windows, touching every surface with fresh, cool, air.

"What happen, kære?" Alf asks a shaky August, holding out their hands to take hers, steadying and grounding.

"Celeste... they... told me..." August tires, the words stuck in her stomach, losing their way, weighty and hurtful, coated in anger and betrayal.

"Take your time, kære, I here when you ready." Alf reassures.

He speaks slowly and softly, as he often does, running his thumbs back and forth over the tops of August's hands, his fingers tucked under her palms, encasing her in fatherly love and patience.

Salt flowing and splashing, as August tries to breathe, to steady herself, to get her words out.

But sticky and indignant they are, battling to remain inside.

Not for fear of judgement or scorn, but for fear of the moment being real, the pain soaking into her bones, eating away at her joy, recolouring her memories.

What would she do then? When the best thing that ever happened, turns out to the most hurtful?

"Dad, Celeste... they told me... they... th-they slept with someone else." August stumbles out, her chest burning, nose running, tears flowing. "And I know maybe I shouldn't even be upset, b-because it's not like-"

Silently, calmly, Alf lifts their hands, bringing August's to their lips, kissing the backs, light stubble brushing against the soft skin, prickly and caring, lowering their

14

face, and pressing hands to sunspot-laced, pale, loving cheeks.

Small. Centred. Comforting.

He looks to his daughter, watching lovingly, knowing perhaps he won't fully understand the context and extent of this hurt, but he has known pain, and can be here for August completely.

The genuine presence, total openness, care in silence. It pulls August from her explanation, from her desire to downplay her emotions, to cut Celeste too much slack for the sake of saving face.

She is hurt, and she's allowed to be.

"I am upset, even if... if, like, logically... maybe I shouldn't be."

"You can be upset, kære, I love you." Alf soothes, words vibrating through their cheek, as the softness rests on August's hand.

She launches into her father's arms, holding him so tight it takes the wind out of his lungs.

Alf wrapping their arms around her, chin on her head, feeling in the tight hold, the amount of dark, heaviness, that is pulling August down.

A cement weight of harm, hanging by a delicate sting.

"Jeg Elsker dig." He repeats.

"Og jeg Elsker dig, Dad."

They hug August as she cries, sinking fingertips into her drenched, pumpkin t-shirt, telling her without words that they're here, right here, and they can take some of the pain, by reminding her she's not alone in it. Silently, with arms winding, and heart open.

The minutes ticking away, her sobbing drifting off into the cool Summer night, the showers giving way to an early darkness, ushering in the black after the downpour, as water flows inside too.

She walked in with the pain, but she let it out in her father's arms.

With dishes still in the sink, shoes left haphazardly by the door, her nose running onto, and rain soaking into, his loose, lilac, linen blouse, here the two are.

The world can wait a little while, as she lets this go. Seen and cared for, by that far too often evasive of gifts: an empathetic parent.

12:52pm 10th January 2011

Nerd Of The Year, 2K10

"Um… Hathor Zaki?" Celeste asks, spinning in August's tangerine desk chair, the colourful room a blur in motion. "Isn't she the one that gets first place in, like… every subject?"

"Yeah!" August replies, looking up from her toenails, neon green polish in hand. "She's so smart, and like, so good at school. And she's… gay… or, lesbian… maybe, or like, queer… I don't know, but she's one of us."

"Oh! I didn't know…" Celeste responds, not sure if they should ask the question burning the tip of their tongue. "Is it like, racist of me to ask if she's like… allowed to be gay?"

"I… don't know…" August answers, pausing her painting for a moment, internally recoiling at Celeste's question, but hoping this can be a teachable moment. "But, I don't think it's like, about being allowed, it's more like, being able to be open and come out… you know?"

"Oh!" Celeste considers, looking up to August's amber ceiling, vibrant and expressive. "Yeah… I guess people are gay and it's like, some religions, or whatever, are like, ok with it or not… but the gay people are still gay."

"…yeah…" August agrees, returning to her nail painting, wondering for a moment, how much more growth Celeste might need to meet her where she is now.

"So... what about Hathor?" Celeste asks, still unsure why August brought her up.

"Oh right! Well, I was thinking we could all go on a friend-date together." August suggests, blowing on her toes. "Like, queer community type of thing."

"Um, yeah, that sounds cool." Celeste agrees, as she often does, despite being hesitant. "What would we all... like, do?"

"Heaps of stuff!" August declares, excited and alight. "We could go to the movies, or...up The Mount... to the park, get Annie's Ice Cream... anything!"

"Yeah, sounds good..." Celeste agrees, swivelling again in August's desk chair. "But, like... would we... have anything in common, or like... have anything to talk about?"

August cringing slightly.

Knowing Celeste doesn't always mean it negatively, doesn't take away the pang of feeling like they don't ever want to do anything she suggests.

"Ok... but also, we won't know... until we all hang out." She replies, half-smiling and half-rejected. "You know?"

Celeste looking around, gaze darting around the mismatched room, full of bright knickknacks, with veronica walls covered in punk band posters, while every ounce of her body is fighting for a 'no', wanting to keep August all to herself, and feeling so sure she won't enjoy hanging out with Nerd Of The Year, Hathor Zaki.

And despite August's efforts to keep her reactions form showing, Celeste can see how much this means to her, and they don't want to upset her. Not now, not ever.

"True…" They agree, focusing cerulean eyes on bistre ones, and smiling falsely. "Worth a try."

"You sure?" August asks, seeing right through Celeste, Mx. Cellophane over here.

"Yeah." Celeste lies, trying another smile, hoping it's more convincing. "A hundred per cent sure."

"Okay…" August replies, not wanting to push it further. "Let's try the once, and if it's not a good fit, we don't have to try again."

"Really?" Celeste asks, far too excitedly.

"Yeah, really." August agrees, taking in every morsel of Celeste's unbridled excitement. "That's the plan."

Naturally, Celeste moves the conversation along, but August is left behind, stewing in the sensation of being both unseen and monitored by Celeste. As though, at times, she's an accessory Celeste wants to keep in a box, and take out whenever they want something to play with.

Despite knowing she's far ahead of her peers, being met with that reality, always leaves her feeling alone. Even here, in her room, with her love.

It should be comfortable, joyous, beautiful, if clunky and awkward, but if often feels like the wonderful moments are massively outweighed by the odd, the slightly sad, or the blatantly negative.

But perhaps hoping for a balanced, honest, romance, is too much for two seventeen-year-olds.

This might be as good as it gets, for someone like her, somewhere like this, somehow out and proud in high school.

11:35am 7th January 2011

The Loneliest Girl

In The World

"Have they been ok?" Isis asks, holding her Motorola Razr between her cheek and shoulder, as she brings a stack of folded pants to a shelf. "Like, for them."

"I mean... they've been whatever." Hathor replies, pacing around her bedroom, knowing she's home alone, but still wary of ever-listening ears. "What about you?"

"Oh, great dodge!" Isis faux-praises, grabbing a stack of shirts. "Pretty good. Not seeing that Simon guy anymore. But otherwise just chillin'."

"Boo, Simon!" Hathor jokes, flopping onto her bed, staring up at the eggshell ceiling, and watching the teak fan spin. "What kind of chillin'?" She asks, excited to live vicariously through her sister.

"Honestly, nothing. That's the best part." Isis answers, settling at her desk. "I just like, did some washing, but I'm just enjoying my housemates being gone, and having... absolutely nothing to do."

"So like me, but without the parents." Hathor half-jokes, pain running over her words, like water over stone, relentless and ever-eroding.

"...yeah." Isis replies, hearing the hurt through the phone, knowing it too well. "So... like, they haven't been ok?"

"I mean, you know what they're both like." Hathor brushes off, sitting up and watching herself in the mirror.

"Yeah, you have it harder, but." Isis tries, hoping the empathy is making its way through the phone. "I was just trying to sneak out and kiss boys, you're having to-
"

"I don't really wanna talk about, Ice." Hathor pushes back, defensive and strong, seeing her thick brow furrowing, immediately relaxing when she spots herself. "I just... really wanna pretend I'm not here, and look forward to a time, very soon, where that'll be my reality, and I can make excuses for not staying after Christmas like you."

A beat. So silent. Loaded to the brim.

"I'm sorry, H." Isis soothes, feeling the remorse of no longer being present to bare some of the viciousness. "I wish I was strong enough to be able to stay longer, and be here for you more in general."

"It's ok, it's just..." Hathor manages, trying with everything not to cry, turning away from her own reflection. "Can you please just tell me about your last few days. I just wanna hear. Anything, please."

"...yeah." Isis's shaky voice comes through, followed by a quiet clearing of the throat. "So... I got up like an hour ago, and I had toast for breakfast, then-"

"Wait, wait, you're going too fast." Hathor states sarcastically, glancing back at herself, with full olive cheeks and twinkling russet eyes, enjoying her grinning reflection much more. "What did you have on the toast? I want *every* detail."

"You're such a little shit." Isis volleys.

"But I'm *your* little shit." Hathor throws back, biting a laugh back.

"...you are." Isis affirms, the smallest chuckle coming through. "You're stuck with me." She soothes, warm like hot chocolate, sweet too.

The lightness filling Hathor instantly, enough to hover, not yet ready to fly, but willing.

Isis retelling the mundane every day of being nineteen, having space to herself, and living off-campus in a share house. Nothing more fascinating to Hathor, biding her time until she can escape this house too.

She could listen for hours. But of course, all too soon Isis has to go, and it's just Hathor and the eggshell walls again.

A book, a CD, or scrolling on Tumblr, only offering so much relief.

The summer holidays seeming to trudge on forever, for the loneliest girl in the world, without a real-life friend, let alone two.

9:41pm 3rd January 2011

It Does Feel Like

Everything Dies In The Summer

It's All Dirt Now

August's heart beating against her ribs, her breath shredding her lungs as it ravages its way through, her footing not always sure, her Volleys slipping on the grey gravel and dry seeds, as she chases Celeste up The Mount.

Giggles, shouts, grunts. The warm summer air dancing with sounds of the engulfing nature.

"Fuck you!" August calls, in between breaths. "I... I'll fucking..."

"Fucking what?" Celeste teases, turning as they reach the top. "You can't do anything until you catch me!"

Celeste swings a leg over the concrete barrier, straddling it, leaning back suggestively.

"Like what you see?"

August throws up a middle finger, steps becoming less sure as she runs out of breath.

"I'll take that as a yes!" Celeste continues, raising an eyebrow. "Come on, slow poke! I wanna kiss you!"

August rolls her eyes at those words.

As if she'd ever turn down Celeste's kisses, as if she ever needs incentive to take Celeste into her arms, to feel Celeste's body against hers, to breathe them in, to taste them, to feel both hearts beat in sync.

"Not fair!" August calls out. Hands on her knees, bent over catching her breath. "You know I'm way less fit now!"

"Well maybe someone shouldn't have broken her leg!" Celeste teases, noticing August catching glances of her exposed thigh. "You like?"

"You can actually fuck off forever!" August calls, picking up her run again, bounding towards her love. "Unless I catch you first!"

"Oh no! Someone save me! I'm about to be fucked off forever!" Celeste yells into the night air, throwing their arms up in faux distress.

August reaches her, placing both hands on that thigh, Celeste bringing her hands down to cover August's, the pair looking into each other's eyes.

Everything around the pair still, not a sound or light or person, for as far as anyone can see.

Just the two of them, hands held, eyes locked.

Celeste leans down slowly, watching August all the while, eyes closing at the very last second, lips connecting softly.

The taste of August filling Celeste's senses. Solo and jellybeans, sweet yet tangy, the softest touch with a little bite.

August tingling all over, out of breath and lost in love.

Tasting Celeste's sour gummies and Pepsi, deep and tart, an ocean so calm on the surface, with dangerous rips lurking underneath.

Celeste pulling back, gesturing for August to join them on the silver barricade. August happily bouncing up, straddling the concrete, bare legs on the abrasive surface, face eager with lust.

Running her hands along August's thighs, Celeste shuffles the pair together, August's legs over hers, chest to chest, hips to hips.

August's head spinning. Absorbed in Celeste's essence, the most magnificent experience in forever.

The thick, barmy, January surrounding the pair, a warm blanket draping over them, hot between them, full of teenage desire and vacant of watching eyes. The only two people in the world.

August swallows hard, breath shaky, eyes wide, hands behind. Afraid to touch, not sure how, but hoping against hope to get the chance.

Celeste seems to read August's mind, a magic trick in the dark, tracing their hands down August's shoulders, past elbows, to wrists, and guiding hungry fingertips to hips.

Lighting shooting through skin, beautiful electricity raging around August's system, timid hands on Celeste, fingers resting on the hunter green linen, feeling the softness underneath, a wonder of the waves and moon.

Celeste closing her eyes, resting her forehead on August's, soaking in the closeness, breath syncing up, decelerando a due.

Tongue tracing their upper lip slowly, inviting, hypnotising, leaning in for another kiss.

August closing the gap excitedly.

The ground beneath falling away, only the two, floating in a boundless plane of technicolour.

Time never starting or beginning, pressing bodies together, kissing passionately, fingerprints marking shoulders, waists, and hips.

Endless, loving, warm, space existing only for these two, only for now, another dimension created just for two.

In the distance, the distinct sound of a car approaching, the flooding light of high-beam crossing into their shared world.

The two landing back on Earth, or worse, back in Bathurst, with school starting soon, and dickhead rubbernecks driving up The Mount, to honk their horns at teenagers pashing on the cement barricades.

Celeste pulling back, chin up, calling incredible excitement into the Summer. Ecstatic thunder.

A honk from strangers? They'll take it.

There really is nothing like being the centre of attention. It doesn't matter who's centre it is.

August beaming, alight with joy. Her kiss made Celeste scream into the night. She must be doing something right.

"That was... really nice." August compliments, gooey and fluttering.

"Yeah." They reply, laughing into the warm black. "The reviews are good!"

The words don't quite sink into August, too rapt in Celeste, dreamy from their kiss. But, within herself, she knows something seems off about that response. An odd tinge deep in her stomach, telling her this didn't go the way it should.

"Let's go get some Maccas!" Celeste announces, wriggling free from the intertwining of legs and arms in a flash, swinging a leg up, over, and off, heading to her car.

"Yeah!" August agrees, following behind excitedly, bounding over the gravel and dead grass, shoes slipping here and there, familiar painful breaths returning. "Not so fast!"

"Slow poke!" Celeste teases, turning and mocking.

The love gone from this joking, instead a tinge of truth seeping in.

August trying her best to catch her breath, and stay upright, present in the night and her body. Wanting only to keep up, to spend time with Celeste, not able to see the cracks forming, to note the difference in delivery.

Screaming songs in cars, talking late into the night, and occasional hot kisses, proving too enamoring for a seventeen-year-old to examine responses and tonal shifts.

3:49pm 12th November 2010

Happy Broken Leg!!

"Hey!" Celeste calls, bursting into August's hospital room, giant 'GET WELL SOON' balloon following. "How are you feeling?"

"...hey..." August replies weakly, drowsy from morphine, shaky smile on her full lips. "...that balloon's... sooo big..."

"Of course! Only the best for my *girlfriend*!" Celeste declares, walking over to the small wardrobe, and tying the balloon to a handle, before turning to August warmly. "Does it hurt?"

"...not a big... I mean... bit..." August laughs, eyes fluttering, barely staying open for a few seconds at a time. "...morphine's great... you should get some... so warm... like a hug through my veins..."

"That's probably why so many World War I soldiers got addicted." Celeste jokes, sitting down in the chair by August's bed. "That and the horrors."

"...the horrors..." August repeats, loopy and amused. "...why you sitting so far away?... I'm dying..."

"What?!" Celeste worries, leaning in.

"...yeah, I'm... dying..." August laughs, squeaky and nasal.

"That's not funny, G!" Celeste protests, sitting up on the hospital bed, lightly tapping August's side in objection. "You're in a fucking hospital, you might be!"

"...nah, I'm not dying..." August folds, laughing along with her words, gesturing for Celeste to lay down with her.

Gently, cautiously, Celeste joins August on the tiny hospital bed, settling into a little spoon position easily, August's hand coming up to brush mousy locks from her ear.

"I'm... never gonna die..." August whispers, laying a playful kiss on Celeste's earlobe.

"You better not." Celeste says softly, wrapped in August's arms and tubes, feeling the cast bump their foot. "I'd miss you too much."

"...oh, what do you...like, love me... or something?" August giggles into Celeste's hair, their glistening face sticking to the strands. "...gay..."

"Of course it's gay." Celeste pushes back, chuckling. "We're gay together. We're gay little queers." She continues, before considering if she should push out those three small words, and deciding she absolutely should. "...And I do... love you."

"Aww... I love you too..." August replies, hugging Celeste tighter, floppy head pressing into the crown of their head. "...who else is gonna... bring me a huge balloon... in my time of need?"

"Literally anyone else!" Celeste jokes, chuckles escaping her thin, peach lips. "I just went to the newsagents and bought it, it was easy."

"...maybe... but you brought it... to me... while I was dying..." August pushes back, speaking gentle words into short mousy hair. "...who else is gonna... do that, hmmm?"

"Ok fine." Celeste relents, smiling warmly. "I guess it could only be me. No one else could possibly."

"...not a soul... in the whole world..." August agrees, laying her cheek on those locks, soft and freshly washed, feeling incredible in the lovesick, morphine-coloured, haze. "...not anyone... else..."

August's eyes closing, heavy and real this time, feeling safe with Celeste in her arms, and relieved to have stayed awake long enough to see them, letting every ounce of determination go, sinking into the now.

The bleach-clean sheets, the scratchy hospital gown, leg encased and safe, serene and dopey, forehead leaning into Celeste, falling into that beautiful liminal space of sleep.

Celeste silently smiling, encased and beloved, unsure if she deserves it, but willing herself to sink into it all the same.

Soft, real, genuine.

Floating on a plane unknowable without August, closing their cerulean eyes for a moment, breathing it in, imprinting it somewhere special, in case it's ever needed.

But of course, Celeste knows, it will be.

9:31pm 4th January 2011

Dr. Faye Tandi,

If Ya (Emotionally) Nasty

A night that had only just kissed the sky, the sun staying well into the evening, painting with brushstrokes of burning heat, so striking as the light finally fades.

Days so long, especially in the silence, without word from Celeste.

August laying on her bed, weary from the waiting, and the baking sun, hoping only to soak in the welcome night.

How fun it had been, how fun it often is, until the slightest move is made, and Celeste recoils swiftly, as though August is made of cursed poison.

She ached to feel Celeste's skin on hers, to touch and taste, the thoughts rushing her mind, as she gladly took any crumbs Celeste gave. Starving and fed only a morsel.

The many nights she placated her hunger alone, wishing, hoping, that one day Celeste would join her, that they could know each other so intimately.

And on the many occasions when she turned that desire inward, it would all too easily end painfully.

Voices circling her head, menacing, asking if Celeste even liked her, even tolerated her presence, or if she'd ever feel true intimacy, because obviously, she is missing out on a life-changing experience.

Sex is so nebulous, so unknowable, without another, without experience, it's only questions, and August is curious.

To hear whispers of how easy it is for her straight peers, the sense that everyone was enjoying something she couldn't seem to know, it left her feeling like she was even more of a weirdo-loser-fuckup.

Not only is she bisexual, but she's not even good at it.

Only seventeen, but with not much else to do in Bathurst, she should know how to fuck like the best of them by now.

She can feel the window closing, the voices from classmates and media, telling her what she's fast becoming: one of the last ones without any experience, and no one wants that.

That has to be right, or why else would everyone be saying it?

August feels the words sinking in, whirling around her head, taking them as gospel.

Streams escaping her eyes, mouth against her pillow, face scrunching, as the blood rushes to her face, lifting raspberry to sit just under her brown skin.

"Tickle?" Faye calls from the door, rapping softly. "Do you want to come join us? We're going to watch a DVD."

August can't reply, her muffled breath heaving, her eyes stinging, it's too much to also try to answer her mother.

"Tickle? Are you ok?" Faye calls again, concern lacing her voice. "Would you like some space?"

August tries to catch her breath, knowing it can be heard through the door.

"Tickle, if you'd like some space, don't say anything, and I'll go."

A beat. Screaming silence through the door.

But she changes her mind.

"...M-Mum..." August pushes, words soaked in tears.

"Should I come in, Tickle?" Faye asks, forehead on the door.

"...yeah..."

A handle turning slowly, a warm Faye appearing in the doorway.

Full lips smiling, fuchsia scarf keeping dark coils off her face, caring, liquorice eyes, shimmering with empathetic tears.

The doctor walks cautiously into her daughter's room, pointing to the desk chair opposite a crying August, silently asking if she can sit here.

August sniffles and nods, wordless and clear.

Faye rolling the chair over to August, sitting down softly, and lifting a hand out to her daughter.

August takes it eagerly, feeling herself fall into the safety of hallowed ground.

That hand is damp and messy, but of no matter to Faye, as she places a palm on top for good measure, and smiles down at August. Her dark skin so warm, her cheeks so full, as though love itself is contained in her face.

"Do you want to talk about it, Tickle?"

August considers the words, unsure if she even has an answer.

She manages a shrug, and looks down. Thankful for the company, but unable to look at her mother right now.

"That's ok, Tickle, we can just sit a little while."

Faye's words float over to August, so loving and patient, unmarred by concepts like changing plans and unpredictable teenage emotions.

The night seeping in, genuine darkness marking the sky now, as the pair soak in the quiet, time feeling insignificant. Maybe it's been three minutes, maybe three hours, but it matters not, for being here is the endeavour of now.

"It's... about s-sex..." August speaks, finally breaking the silence.

"That's ok, Tickle, we can always talk about sex." Faye comforts, leaning in, warm and open. "Do you have new questions? Or is it something from earlier?"

"Maybe... both? It's more that... like, am I a loser if I haven't had sex yet?"

August looks to her mother, wanting to watch words being formed in real time, hoping to catch hidden meaning in facial expressions.

Faye smiles and nods slowly, considering August's concealed meaning.

"Hmm, that's a tough one, Tickle, there will unfortunately always be people who call you names regardless of your choices." Faye begins, looking lovingly into August's bistre eyes. "But your choices are your own, and all you can do, is make the best decision at the time, with the information you have. And I'm always here, as is your father, if you have questions."

August nods, the cool tears on her pillow rubbing against her hot cheeks, grounding contrast.

"When did you first have sex?" She asks, looking into those loving, liquorice eyes.

Faye takes in a cooling breath, and lets out a heavy sigh.

"Well, the context was very different for me, Tickle." She replies, squeezing August's hand. "One of the reasons my parents left Zimbabwe, was because they were concerned for my sexual safety."

"Oh." August shrinks, guilt panging her insides.

"No… Tickle, don't worry about me. It's why I went into gynaecology." Faye replies, squeezing again, smiling warmly. "It's just that… it was a different story for me. Sex wasn't the rite of passage it is now, not in Zimbabwe at least, and certainly not in my parent's eyes."

August retreating at her mother's words. Avoiding eye contact, shrinking her body up, knowing her mother isn't trying to shame her, but feeling remorse regardless.

"Tickle, talk to me." Faye says simply. "Or would you like some space?"

"No!" August calls, before realising her raised voice, and retracting somewhat. "No, I'd like to keep talking. It's just, I feel bad... because it was so different for you, and I didn't consider that."

"Oh, Tickle... it isn't your burden to worry about me. I'm the parent. I worry about you."

August sits up, hands squeezing fiercely, and with fresh tears flowing down her cheeks, collapsing into her mother's arms.

"...Tickle..." Faye comforts, pulling August onto her lap, and into a tight, loving hug.

Eyes closed. Grip warm. Adoration heavy.

"I don't think Celeste likes me..." August murmurs, salt cascading down, and into Faye's kaftan.

"Tickle, what makes you say that?" Faye asks, gentle fingers running over August's dark curls.

"They... hardly ever touch me..." August stumbles, words leaking tears. "And we started kissing yesterday... but they pulled away when this car came past and, like... haven't even texted me or anything."

August sobs into the azure fabric of Faye's house dress, unsure if she's seeing something that isn't there, or not seeing something that's hilariously obvious.

"Aww, Tickle... I'm sorry, that's confusing." Faye comforts, rubbing August's back, as it heaves. "And this is a confusing time already. I'm sorry that you were sitting her alone, all day, with these feelings."

"No, I needed... some time to like, process... or something." August replies, recalling her day staring at veronica walls.

"Yes, sometimes time alone is good too." Faye comforts, pressing open palms into August's back, holding her daughter closer for a beat. "But I'm sorry to say, Tickle, you may need to be the bigger person and bring this up with Celeste. They might not have the support you have, and they might need you to be that support."

"Oh." August responds, pulling back enough to look her mother in the eye.

It's warmth. It's affection. It's support.

Faye nods, August resting a cheek on Faye's shoulder. Close, caring, compassionate.

"And maybe they're just not ready for a sexual relationship." Faye continues, the words vibrating through her chest to August. "So, you might have to decide if you're willing to be that support for them, while also remembering that giving love isn't a transaction."

"...yeah..." August breathes, shaking as she tries to steady herself.

"You might pour a lot of love into Celeste, and they might not return it, Tickle." Faye reassures, drawing circles between August's shoulder blades. "That doesn't mean they're not trying their hardest, it just means they don't have the same tools you have."

Faye's words drift into August's ears, and seep into her brain, deep into the tissue, planting seeds, germinating and ruminating.

She sniffles a response, a small gesture to let her mother know she's listening.

"And you don't have to do anything right now, or even tomorrow. But I think you do need to talk to them, not just make assumptions and hurt yourself."

August nods, knowing her mother will feel it in the loving hold.

"But for now, would you like to come join Alf and me?" Faye asks, tightening the squeeze one last time. "Or would you like some time by yourself, Tickle?"

August takes in the last squeeze, then leans back enough for her mother to cradle shaky shoulders in loving palms, watching and waiting.

"Yeah, it'd be nice to come hang out with you and dad." She nods, sniffling.

Faye gently reaches up to run a caring thumb over August's soaked cheek.

"Alright. I'll go wash up and grab you some Panamax, wash up if you like, and come join us when you're ready." Faye reassures, gently pinching August's chubby cheek, eliciting a soft smile. "Ndinokuda, Tickle. We can talk again any time, okay?"

August nods, reaching for some tissues, as Faye leans to kiss her forehead, slow and calm, breathing her in.

Adoring. Appreciating. Affectionate.

"Ndinokudawo, Mum." August replies, dabbing her eyes.

7:39pm 13th January 2011

It's Called

Being A Lesbian, DUH!

"I'm sorry, by the way." Celeste says, looking anywhere but Hathor, recalling spending Tuesday with her. "I was... super weird that day."

"Oh, ok." Hathor replies, unsure if she actually wants to resolve this, or pretend that friend-date didn't happen. "I mean, I was just happy to hang out, so..."

"Well, you know, it was cool to hang out." Celeste nods, stiff and awkward, reaching for her bracelets, anything to busy herself.

"Totally." Hathor replies, craning her neck, enviously looking over Celeste's collection of trinkets, from her spot on the beige armchair by the closed door. "It's cool to hang out with other gay people, so... yeah."

"When did you know?" Celeste asks, turning to Hathor as they pull on three hot pink elastic bracelets, and look over their reflection in the large mirror on their wardrobe door.

The emotional whiplash hitting Hathor where she sits, with one leg up, on the armchair. Her canary 'I'M NOT GAY BUT MY BOYFRIEND IS' slogan tee, unintentionally concealed by her grape leggings, as

41

she's rendered speechless by the sudden subject change.

But as a guest, she doesn't want to seem rude, and as she feels her thick brows furrowing, tries to relax the muscles, instead flashing a smile up at a waiting Celeste.

"That I'm a lesbian?" Hathor answers with her own question, feeling at odds with the intrusiveness, and relief from the previous staleness.

"Yeah." Celeste affirms, assuming this is what queer people talk about, while hanging out at each other's houses.

Hathor blinking russet eyes up at a clueless Celeste, not sure if she prefers the standoffish version from Tuesday, or this oddly familiar one, but curious to see where this goes.

"When I was about three or four-"

"That young?" Celeste interrupts, cerulean eyes wide, mousy brows high.

"Yeah!" Hathor joyfully declares, Celeste's room fading from view, as treasured images dance into her mind's eye. "I still have this really clear memory of my friend's older sister in, like, a graphic tee, with like, a knock-off Simpson's design on it, and denim cut-off shorts, helping me up when I fell off my bike..."

The words wafting over to Celeste, painting the picture in the walls of their mind, crafting the image as though the memory was theirs too. A loud voice wishing it was.

"...and it was like, the sun was behind her." Hathor continues, the moment so clear, projecting inside her skull, timeless and precious. "And she had these prominent freckles, and this like, thick red hair, it kind of, blocked the sun, like she was more important than the whole sun, or something..."

"...fuck." Celeste breathes, bathing in the potency of Hathor's words.

"Yeah." Hathor nods, smiling to herself, the vision playing on loop, an enchanted cinemagraph.

Celeste frozen in place, thumb tracing their elastic bracelets, watching Hathor intently, feeling an intangible sensation, knowing something is shifting, but not being sure what precisely.

Feeling eyes on her, Hathor glances up to Celeste, instantly blinking back guilt, as she feels those cerulean eyes burning into her, recognising that look anywhere.

"And I knew." Hathor shrugs, hoping to deflect that gaze, and the desire behind it. "I liked girls, and like, pretty much only girls." Hathor sneaking a peek to see if her implied meaning is caught, before throwing the focus off herself. "What about you?"

"I mean... I guess... I still... don't, um... kn-know for sure." She replies, turning back to her wardrobe, pretending to search for something, anything.

Celeste has it. Clear now. They're feeling the coral rushing to their pale cheeks, the heat rising in their ears, the flutter in their middle.

So, this is what it's supposed to feel like.

"That's ok." Hathor soothes, sitting forward in the armchair, forearms crossing over canary tee and grape leggings, glad to have the attention off her.

"It is?" Celeste asks, charade of wardrobe rummaging pausing, focus back to Hathor, gaze falling low, hoping their arousal won't be perceived.

"Um... yeah. Obviously." Hathor assures, knowing this doesn't have to be anything of note to anyone, it's simple, the most natural and boring thing in the world. "No everyone is gonna know right away. And you could be bi."

Celeste absorbs Hathor's words, turning slowly, eyes flitting, sneaking glances here and there of a watchful olive face, warmth radiating.

"How... would I know?" They ask, fingers squeezing their bare thighs nervously, wondering if their ignorance or attraction was more obvious, and hoping it was neither.

"Well, you know you're nonbinary, right?" Hathor guides, remaining forward, a gesture of hearing, of seeing, of being present.

And seeing she absolutely is.

"Yeah." Celeste shrugs, unsure where Hathor is leading her, but willing to follow all the same.

"I guess it's the same." Hathor continues, dots connecting like stars in the night sky. "Does bisexual feel... right? Like, as good a fit as nonbinary?"

Celeste considering for a moment, becoming less steady, stepping over to their desk chair, hoping to find grounding.

Hathor following with only eyes, as they pass her, noting those bare legs for a flicker, and only a flicker, russet eyes returning to a pale face.

Settling into the scratchy ballet pink seat, Celeste breathes a heavy burden, the material prickling into her thighs, with navy linen shorts providing no protection.

Celeste internally cursing the chair, another item forced on them by the slow, insidious, nightmare that is Lydia Breadseed.

"Hmm... maybe?" They finally answer, heavy palms on knees, eyes to Hathor, but pale face forward.

"I feel like that's a 'no'." Hathor replies, body turning to face Celeste, crossing legs and resettling elbows on the chair's arm. "A 'maybe' is just a 'no', I reckon so, anyway."

The revelation hits Celeste with importance. She might not completely understand why right now, but it burrows into her brain for safekeeping.

"Oh. I guess it might be." They agree, hauntings of every 'maybe' they gave their mother, flashing like a camera in the night, bringing that which is hidden in darkness, into the light.

"But like, are there any men that you... like?" Hathor follows up, hands gesturing, curious and warm, adding an air of gossip, rather than interrogation. "Even as an idea?"

She watches Celeste think her question over, enjoying the way their thin, peach lips part slightly, how their mousy, thin brows furrow, and their eyes move side to side, like they're reading at superspeed.

But what they're reading, is the real mystery.

"Um, like… Crispin Glover." Celeste replies, swivelling side to side slightly, eyes on her misty rose ceiling. "But like, only in the Charlie's Angeles movies. He's like… weird, and I'm like… yeah."

"That is the most lesbian answer to that question." Hathor jokes, head lolling forward in emphasis. "Like…"

"Is it?" Celeste asks, taken aback, focus snapping to Hathor.

"Yeah." Hathor affirms, slamming palms to her leggings, with an expression of amused confusion. "Characters like Creepy Thin Man are like… 'gender-defying' in a way that's like… lesbian-hot."

Celeste resuming their swivelling to think over Hathor's assertion, trying to calibrate how it fits into their point-of-view, if at all.

"Ok, yeah, I see that." Celeste agrees, halting their swivelling, to ask: "But also… what about nonbinaries?"

She sneaks a glance to Hathor, wanting her meaning to sink in, to be heard, without having to outright ask. Because that would cause her to completely fade away.

"I mean… would 'lesbian' include nonbinaries in *your* eyes?" Hathor enquires, hoping to ensure there's not a trace of pretence or embarrassment in her tone, while also aiming to avoid Celeste's implicit question. "If it was the word *you* used?"

"Maybe." Celeste shrugs, disappearing into themself, arms crossing over their honeydew shirt, taking the small rejection right to the veins, pumping through their system like poison.

"So, that's another no." Hathor comforts, half-smiling at a deflating Celeste, wanting to keep on the topic at hand.

She can see it though, the effect her deflection has. Celeste isn't entirely hiding it that well. But she's just trying to make friends, and keeping conversations platonic might have to be the hill she dies on today.

"Yeah… no." They nod, sitting up slightly, willing the poison away, as they often do.

"Well, what about sapphic?" Hathor follows up, bringing her tone back to simple enquiry, putting her platonic plan into action. "That's a bit more… it's got more wiggle room."

"…I don't think so… it feels a bit… academic." Celeste pushes back, trying her best to find an evasive 'no' once again, and keep that poison down. "It's named after the poet, right?"

"Queer? Just 'queer'?" Hathor asks, unphased by Celeste's pushes, genuinely interested in exploring and helping, feeling more comfortable in a more abstract conversation, at least for her. "It's been an old faithful since like… the 60's."

"How… do you know all these words?" Celeste questions, feeling simultaneously supported and ignorant to their own identity.

"The internet, duh." Hathor laughs, shrugging playfully, relieved to be able to find a punchline. "And there's not much to do at my house." She explains, smile turning to a smirk. "But on my laptop… I can pretend I'm doing schoolwork, my parents don't know."

Celeste sighs, looking up at their misty rose ceiling, feeling the pang of jealousy drift over their body. Perhaps they could be educated on queer identity as well, if only they weren't absolutely terrified of their parents monitoring their every move, and scolding at any steps outside the unspoken lines.

Hathor looking over Celeste's room in the short lull, wondering what it must be like to be this well-off.

Sure, The Breadseeds weren't flashy about their wealth. Lydia teaches Law at Charles Sturt University, but here, in a regional centre. The family has three top-of-the-line cars with all the extra features, but they're reasonable, well-maintained, Holdens. Timothy travels for work every other week, but who doesn't, in a country this large?

Celeste doesn't even go to one of the three private schools in this education town. And not just because one of them wouldn't even have her.

Still, they are more than comfortable. Someone to cook and clean for your family, a bedroom this immaculate, everything matching and new, never going without, all because your father is the heir to moderately successful, UK-based, Breadseed Records.

It's hard for Hathor not to enviously think: 'it must be nice'.

Especially sitting here in an op-shop tee and Best&Less leggings. Sure, she'll fight a bear in a nightclub for the tee, but being able to buy something new and high-quality feels as impossible as being A Heterosexual Housewife.

"I feel a bit... uneducated in this area." Celeste admits, looking back to Hathor, and returning to the conversation and the now.

There's a tiny jump Hathor feels in her body, unaware she had drifted so far, and the snap back jolting through her somewhat unpleasantly, all too used to repressing her flinches.

"I mean, you know who Sappho was, you're not that uneducated." Hathor reassures, trying to keep her tone even, with a sprinkle of levity. "And it would be ok if you were. Queer history has been destroyed like a bunch of times, it's something we have to like, actively seek out. It's like a rite of passage or something."

She smiles, willing it to come off caring and real, as she leans in again, forearms returning to thighs, awaiting Celeste's reply.

"What's it like at your house?" They ask, leaning in too, and slowly walking the desk chair closer. "Like, with the lesbian stuff?"

"It's weird..." Hathor begins, noting Celeste edging closer, and internally fighting between relishing it and detesting herself for that relish. "My parents are impossible enough without coming out to them, but I think they like, know." She continues, russet gaze flicking to the ever-closing gap. "I think sometimes me being like, Muslim Lite was a bigger deal than my queerness."

"Oh." Celeste replies, almost knee-to-knee with Hathor, curious to know more, see more, feel more. "Can I... ask more about... your religion?"

"Yeah, but, there's not much to say." Hathor responds, rolling her knee over slightly, touching Celeste's to hers, the electricity radiating through the small contact, spiders' webs of desire. "The way my parents talk about it, is like they assumed I would, I dunno... want to fit in or something. Like, not be Egyptian, just be Aussie." She explains, slowly sliding her forearms down grape leggings, that spider's web screaming for more. "And it's like, as though they both think me being a lesbian is... trying to fit in?"

Forearms reaching knees, Hathor unfurling an index finger to graze Celeste's calf, measured and clear. All the while watching for any sign that she should pull back, and hoping for another bold gesture from Celeste in kind.

A sharp breath in response.

Celeste breathing out, and leaning in, extending a finger to stroke along Hathor's.

Dangerous. Betraying. Irresistible.

It's too much and not enough. Scratching an itch that needs to be sanded to the cartilage.

"What about your parents?" Hathor breathes, curling that finger up to hold Celeste's digit, breathing deep and slow, as though any sudden movements would break the magical trance. "They're English, right?"

"So fucking English." Celeste replies, laced with ulterior meaning. "It's bad sometimes. Their like, 'we're not gonna talk about it' bullshit makes me so fucking angry." They continue, moving in closer again, forehead hovering a hair from Hathor's, pulsing with galvanic craving. "Always talking about me like I'm not

in the room. Whether it's about gay shit or like, exams…
it's always like I'm this thing that they pass around and
talk about."

"That's rough." Hathor soothes, bridging the tiny gap,
foreheads touching, breathing in, feeling light enough
to float up to the misty rose ceiling, and bathe in the
colour, like the fountain of youth. "And who do you talk
to about that?"

"What do you mean?" Celeste asks, eyes closing,
soaking in the intimacy, feeling it recolour everything
it touches, like sunlight caroming rainbows all over
bedroom walls.

"Like, do you talk to August about it?" Hathor asks,
barely feeling the meaning of the words as they leave
her full lips.

The question eliciting a swift pull back from Celeste,
guilt stitching misery into the lining of their insides.

"Or… Have you found any community or friends
online?" Hathor continues, unmoving in the face of
Celeste's sudden change, not wanting to show the
internal hurt and concern.

"No. Have you?" Celeste asks, picking at the navy linen
in her lap, suddenly fascinated by her own shorts.

"Uh, yeah." She answers, pulling up slowly, creating
space between her and Celeste, a chasm where a
moment ago there was unity. "There's a queer Arab
community I found on Tumblr about a year ago. I
follow a bunch of them, and go on there most days, it's
like memes and stuff or people talking about their
families." Hathor continues, feeling the warmth re-
enter her soul, thinking of the joy and affirmation she's

51

found in the ones and zeroes of the World Wide Web. "There's a lot of us. No one here, but... we exist. If we're out or not."

Her own sentiment sinking in for a second, a strong bittersweetness starting in her teeth, running through the nerves, behind her eyes, and deep into her brain.

What wonder that she, a random teen in country NSW, is able to feel less alone. But what tragedy that so many have spent so much longer in perilous isolation. No one to extend a hand, saying 'you can be yourself with us'.

The thought spinning her head into another dimension, not new, but ever powerful, as though she holds that suffering in her young body.

"I hadn't thought about that." Celeste speaks, bringing Hathor back to the neutral, muted, bedroom. "Not even talking to G."

"Oh." Hathor replies, trying her best to find her consciousness, and plug it into her body. "But isn't she like... your girlfriend?"

"Yeah." Celeste nods, moving her fiddling to the hot pink bracelets on her pale wrist.

"Well, some people... talk to their girlfriends when they're sad and need to like... get stuff off their chests." Hathor explains, willing her tone to stay matter-of-fact, and not drip with judgement.

"Oh."

"What are you just like..." Hathor continues, hoping to inject some humour. "Fucking all the time?"

She can see it, her joke catapulting from her teeth, and slain in mid-air. Falling onto the crème carpet, dead on impact.

"We... haven't." Celeste replies, eyes low, watching their own fiddling with fascination.

"But I thought you two had been together since like... third term." Hathor digs, mouth moving too fast to filter her words, only her tone, and just enough to come across as curious, not malicious. "What's that... six months? Are you... not into that?"

"I don't know." Celeste admits, feeling at ease here, as though talking with Hathor is magically easier. "The idea is really sexy, and when she looks at me it's like 'oh this is on!', but when we're touching it's like 'does this feel good?' you know?"

Nodding along out of sheer politeness, and for something to keep her from displaying emotions too clearly, Hathor hears Celeste, and does everything in her power not to widen her eyes, or raise her dark brows. Yet somehow, it comes through anyway.

"Is that bad?" Celeste panics, the ease leaving as quickly as it walked in.

"Not necessarily." Hathor reassures, meaning it. "Especially if you're not ready."

"But I do, like... get horny just not... for her." Celeste speaks, thoughts verbalising before they can be sifted through the brain. "Oh fuck! That's so awful! That's so fucked of me to say!"

Defeated head falling into waiting pale palms, short mousy locks bobbing forward, providing a small and crucial shelter.

"I mean, it's not, if it's... true." Hathor reassures, reaching a tentative hand out to lay lightly on Celeste's shoulder, fingertips tracing over the cool, light, bamboo rayon.

With forehead to palms, Celeste feels Hathor's touch, glancing through her fortress of short hair, keen to take anything she can get.

"I mean..." Hathor continues, drawing soothing touches over honeydew bamboo. "What attracted you to August?"

"She's... she's the best, and so patient and like..." Celeste scrambles, fighting to stay focused on the discussion, with tingles radiating from Hathor's fingers. "I don't know, makes me want to be better."

"That's great stuff. That's really great." Hathor replies, slowing her tracing, something telling her the beeswax of her feathered wings is melting. "But... do you like kissing her and stuff?"

"I mean... it feels nice, but maybe not... hot." Celeste elaborates, not sure if they're talking only about August or also about someone much closer.

"Right." Hathor responds, pulling her hand back slowly, not wanting hubris to have her falling to the sea. "And what do you think that means?"

"You're the label expert." Celeste replies, a small trace of humour in her words, as she curls her fingers and puts chin to palms instead, glancing to Hathor. "What do you think?"

"I think..." Hathor responds, sitting deep in the beige armchair, trying to keep distance between her and The Sun. "It's not ok for me to tell you about your own relationship."

The sentiment being true, but not the answer Celeste was wanting after.

Cerulean eyes darting to the crème carpet, leaning back in the scratchy ballet pink desk chair, sudden distance created.

Hathor seeing it, feeling both reassured and rejected. Wondering if Celeste was backing off for the same reason she was.

No time for much contemplation as the door opens behind Hathor.

"Thanks for waiting!" August chimes, slipping in, face flushed from the heat, breathing a sigh of relief to be inside, with the nice air-con.

"Of course, yeah." Celeste replies, sitting bolt upright, trying to push down the last few minutes. "It was no worries, right Hathor?"

"None at all!" Hathor asserts, a little too loud to be inconspicuous.

August standing in between, looking from Celeste to Hathor, and back again, hands on hips, bistre eyes squinting.

"Did you two get along?" She accuses, smiling like a painter admiring their finished portrait.

"What-?"

"W-we-"

"You did!" August declares, happy with her handywork. "This is the best!"

Celeste and Hathor trying to protest, and August playfully brushing both off, instead insisting they must both be hungry since they've been 'talking mad shit for ages', she's sure.

Ushering both out, grabbing bags and donning shoes on the way out, they all load into August's hatchback, as she continues to silence protests, and they all head to Red Rooster. Her shout.

3:12pm 29th December 2010

All Messed Up by The Donnas

"What if... what if in the new year we... um" August tries, heart pounding, mind racing, salacious images clouding her vision.

"If we... what?" Celeste teases, turning to face August.

They move across their bedroom, an angel floating on clouds, illuminated by the pounding light of the stretching afternoon, ethereal and enamouring.

August completely consumed in the sight. Speechless and frozen.

"If we what, G?" Celeste breathes, soft and commanding.

August swallows hard, the question is right there, hanging in the air, if only she can reach out and grab it.

Celeste tilts her head, smiling, riding high on the sensation of causing such speechlessness.

A special skill, sacred and unknowable to most. But they, with grin so devilish, and eyes that demand attention, can pull it out any time they like.

How the time slows, August's words lost in the shade, unable to come to the light.

Celeste breathes a single letter, the 'G' circling around August, a house in a hurricane, lifted and orbiting, absorbed into the chaos.

They lean down, staring lover's daggers into August's bistre eyes, close but so far. Barely a breath between faces.

Lips ready, eyes fixed, butterflies dancing, not a single thought. Only here, only now, Celeste living up to their name. Heavenly, otherworldly, and out of reach.

Too powerful for August, and she's falling once again, into Celeste, deeper still.

Celeste can feel it. That moreish sensation of sweet adoration, the power of infatuation, the absolute gift of irresistibility.

They know it well. It's new, but it fits like a glove. A way to feel unstoppable, untouchable, and most of all, unknowable.

For the pull is strong enough to halt anything in its tracks, chew it up, and spit it out.

And they wield it whenever they please, the ultimate trump card.

"Did you have a question, G?" Celeste asks, brushing her nose against August's.

No time for a speechless August to answer, as Celeste closes the gap, landing a soft, magnificent kiss on waiting lips.

Head spinning, mind fogging, stomach dropping.

Celeste pulling back, the promised land just out of reach again.

"Hmm?"

"I... don't..." August tries, thoughts taken, question gone, images long forgotten. "I-I..."

"Maybe later." Celeste teases, straightening, turning, sauntering back to her wardrobe.

Walking on air, the only magical one, living for the effect they have on August, a shot right to the brain, running through their pathways, sinking into cartilage, tendons, and ligaments, diving and soaking.

She smiles, enjoying the sensation as she resumes her search for that tiffany blue and periwinkle ombre shirt, another object picked out for her by Lydia, and acquired by Timothy, on yet another business trip.

Celeste silently questioning, as they rummage for that storied shirt, if sex with August could ever be as good, as wielding the power to captivate her.

August watching the hovering figure. Ethereal, grace personified, the most spellbinding being in this or any universe, even when simply rummaging in their wardrobe, for something to wear to the movies.

But perhaps, if she can't even talk about sex and intimacy, likes and dislikes, she probably isn't ready to get jiggy with it. Even with someone she's known for so many years.

But as Celeste's massive wardrobe as her witness, she'd saw her foot off in an underground bathroom, with a puppet watching, just for the chance.

12:03am 15th January 2011

Please Don't Talk To Me,

I Just Want To Have A Shower,

And Go To Bed

"How was the movie, Pumpkin?" Jamila asks, as Hathor tries to sneak past her mother.

"It was good, yeah." Hathor hastily replies, hoping to wrap this up quickly and go. "The best I've ever seen."

"Really? Hmmm…" Jamila lightly prods, lowering her glasses, as she looks up for her solitaire. "You know, it's a good thing you're only going to the movies with friends."

Hathor knows better than to argue.

It never got her anywhere, and any valid points are always dismissed as 'disrespect'. Instead, she's learned to simply force herself to reply 'ok', and keep the sheer rage slightly under the surface.

But her plan doesn't work this time.

"Pumpkin!" Jamila calls, just as Hathor thinks she's home free.

She rolls her eyes, taking in a calming breath, and putting on a brave smile, before returning to the dining room, standing in the doorway.

But Jamila doesn't look up from her cards this time.

"Yes?" Hathor prompts, hands behind her back, anticipating something else dismissive or even, downright awful.

"You went with Celeste?" Jamila enquires, looking over her cards as she speaks. "Celeste Breadseed, yes?"

"Um... yeah?"

"Don't say 'yeah' to your mother, I'm not one of your little friends." Jamila snaps, looking up to Hathor with furious anger in her sepia eyes. "Is Celeste a Breadseed or not?"

"Yes, Mum, she is." Hathor replies, knowing that using 'they' would just prolong this conversation. "Why do you ask?"

"Well... Have you spoken to her about... employment?" Jamila elaborates, taking off her glasses, placing them down with gentle, yet controlled intention. "It would look good on your resume."

Her simmering, cold expression looking to a stiff, wary Hathor, as though this idea should have already been executed, despite this being the first time she's suggested it.

"Oh... um, it might be a bit weird working for my classmate's father-"

"Don't talk back, Pumpkin. Celeste is English, she can afford to be picky, not you." Jamila interrupts, tone

61

cruel in its dismissiveness. "Next time, you ask her about working there, maybe in accounting, you're very good with numbers, aren't you?"

"Yes, Mum." Hathor replies, clenching fists behind her back. "That's a great idea, and I'll ask... her... next time."

"Very good." Jamila responds, picking up her glasses, and returning her gaze to the cards. "And don't think that you'll get this much free time when school starts up again. And you won't be allowed out this late *if* you're allowed to start dating."

This. Underhanded. Snake.

Hathor catches the additional meaning: the implied reprimanding for staying out an extra hour.

Jamila loves that move. She never has to be the one who's upset, if she never actually says it.

Deep breath. Hands clenched. Smile wide.

"Of course." Hathor evenly pushes out, sticky indignation bubbling just under the surface. "I'm going to get to bed, it's late."

"Mmm, yes, goodnight." Jamila waves, not looking up.

"Goodnight."

Hathor walks as calmly as possible. The anger urging its way out. Just a little further. And she'll be in the bathroom. She can make it.

Heavy breath. Eyes closed. A few more steps.

Hand on the doorknob. Hurried. She rushes in.

Locking the door behind her. Burying her face in her towel. Shoving the fibres in her mouth. Muffled screams finally flowing. Quiet and violent.

One of few salvations in this house.

Body relaxing, anger deflating, towel returning to the hook, turning taps, water running, face meeting herself in the mirror.

It's all there, still there, same dark chestnut waves, same olive skin, same thick, dark eyebrows, same almond eyes, same rich russet irises.

She thought she'd look different, but she's still the same Hathor, just another seventeen-year-old who fucked in the back of a car.

Steam envelopes the vision, and she shakes from the wonderings.

After turning on the fan, she undresses and steps into the shower, the warm water running down her newly storied skin, covered in a mix of perfume and sweat, the scents circling her in the small glass box.

A part of her wishing that she could marinade in the mixture for the rest of eternity, but the loudest, logical voice, screaming that she can't walk around the house smelling like teenage lust.

The sex replaying, bringing a genuine smile to her lips, as she absentmindedly soaps the washcloth and scrubs herself down, reacquainting herself with her body after sharing it with another.

At times like this it feels maddening. The secrets, the falsehoods, the excuses. The utter painting herself into a corner, that is having to hide so many facets, in whatever cracks she can find, in this house's egg shell walls.

But the true horror, the real flood of fury, comes from the reality that the people who should be her most trusted place, didn't want to know her at all, they merely want her to fulfil a role they've already outlined, they want her to be the idea of herself, which they hold unspoken in their minds.

It seems too great an aspiration, to wish her parents could just see her for who she is. To hope at some point, she wouldn't have to hide such a large part of her, that she could be seen as whole, as beautiful and divine, for who she is, completely.

But, in the January of today, she can't be out and proud.

And she can't pretend to be straight either.

So, she only gets stolen glances, kisses in the back of the cinema, and sex in a car, under the summer night. And it's wonderful and real and heart-warming, but she can't share it with the people who moved mountains for her to exist, to have the privilege of living in this country. Those whose hopes and dreams for her, weigh on her mind like an anvil, crushing her slowly, down into the tiles of a shower, and through the metal of the drain, after a joyous, freeing, hook-up.

12:08am 15th January 2011

I Wish I Could Explode

My Shithead Parents

With My Fucking Mind

"How was the film, Darling?" Lydia asks, uncharacteristically meeting Celeste at the door, and with a smile too.

Lydia standing by the shoe rack, hands on hips, tapping her beslippered foot, looking Celeste up and down, with knives in her cerulean eyes, and seething wrath behind her smile.

"It was... amazing." Celeste answers, not picking up on their mother's underlying scorn, too busy putting keys back in their beige, leather handbag, among the BlackBerry, vermillion Olympus camera, and Nivea Strawberry Lip Care.

"How wonderful!" Lydia falsely assures, passive-aggression coming through in full force. "And did you think it was 'amazing' to stay out an extra hour?"

Celeste's attention snapping up, a familiar alertness rushing their veins.

"Oh, I didn't-"

"You absolutely didn't, Darling." Lydia scolds, cutting through Celeste's words with vicious ease. "I'm so glad you want to give me a heart attack, worrying myself sick, waiting up until midnight for you."

"I-I... I'm sorry, I-"

"You should be sorry. The twins never behaved like this!" Lydia continues, taking an axe to Celeste's attempts to apologise. "You said the film would finish at ten thirty, and here you are, walking in after midnight. Where have you been?"

"W-well... we went to g-get food, and-"

"Junk food!" Lydia exclaims, throwing her hands and head up, disapproval oozing out of every pore. "We've spoken about you putting that poison in your body, it's bad enough you eat that popcorn."

"B-but it's only d-during the holidays-"

"It's starts as 'just the holidays' and next thing you know, you're never taking care of yourself." Lydia berates, leaning in for maximum effect, just inches from Celeste's trembling lip, forcing words out through gritted veneers. "And I am not going to have some dyke heffer for a daughter. Ok?"

"...ok." Celeste replies, tiny and trying to keep from crying.

This woman will never see Celeste shed a tear. Not as long as they live. And they plan to outlive this tyrant if it's the only thing they ever achieve.

"Good." Lydia relents, standing up, looking over Celeste with contempt. "Turn off the lights before you go to bed."

Lydia taking her leave, Celeste frozen in place, hearing the soft, yet angered, footsteps head down the entrance corridor, and up the stairs, her mother muttering under her breath the whole way. A trail of everything Celeste wasn't, left in her wake.

The most vile breadcrumbs.

Back against the wall. In for four. Hold for three. Out for four.

Not here. She's not having a panic attack in the mudroom, with the coats, umbrellas, and shoes, stinking of sweat and a dozen different perfumes and colognes, drowning in the words of her mother.

Nails digging into bare thighs. Eyes closing. Heavy breath in. Hold it. Out slowly.

It's ok. It's all ok. They can do this.

Kicking off her dirty, white Converse, she heads down the corridor, flicking the light off, and standing in the darkness, feeling the familiar helplessness for a short pause.

There are only enemies and bullies in this house.

One hand on the banister, the other on a thigh, pressing a hand into the flesh, pushing as they go, floppy feet plopping onto step after step, slow and defeated.

What beauty, what freedom, just an hour ago, and what a rough landing.

It's all ruined now. They should just head to bed.

Slumping to her bedroom, fingers on the doorknob, turning slowly, not wanting to make a single sound, lest they get another lashing.

She's done it a thousand times, but it still has her heart beating in her throat, ears alert, jaw clenching, neck tense, shoulders tight, wishing against everything, for no indication of that woman, or even worse, that man.

Slow. Measured. Nipping inside.

Back against the door. Sweet safety. Heavy breath out.

Eyes closing, sliding down, knees to chin, arms wrapping around shins, tears streaming.

They can cry here.

Silently. Alone. Scared as all fuck.

Knees shaking, hand over mouth, shoulders tight, rivers flowing from stinging cerulean eyes.

Fingers reaching into the beige handbag, rummaging in the dark, pulling out a camera. Turning on, selecting Review Image, and staring into the pixels.

Longing to be there again, holding it to close, wanting only to step into the image.

Kissing Hathor's cheek, in the back of the Metro 5, flash flooding light into the midnight of the cinema and the image on Celeste's digital camera.

She's been here a thousand times, wishing her present away. Not after such a wonderful night. But it's an evening of firsts after all.

11:16am 31st January 2011

Wow.

Being Back At School.

My Fave.

There she is. Laughing.

Head back, face scrunching, arms up.

That harsh, February sun, lighting her beautifully. Her brown skin glowing under its rays. Her dark, bistre eyes illuminating to the richest golden.

And all Celeste can do is watch.

August laughing, glowing. The girl she cheated on. Happy and free.

The jealousy bubbling inside them. Scorching their insides with its bile.

She had to look away. Run away. Legs carrying her, before her head caught up to where those legs were taking her.

It was a special spot. Or, they guess, it used to be.

Under the Eucalyptus trees, behind the oval, in the dip before the fence.

Perfectly hidden. Among nature. Sacred and secluded.

Celeste throwing her bag down, falling to her knees, bottle green school skirt crumpling between calves and thighs, instant grass stains on white socks. And the organic, cleansing, subtle scent of Eucalyptus, embracing her all around.

Feeling so much, their thoughts so scattered, not one thing clear, and certainly not ready to voice a single idea to another person, especially not August.

What could she say? How could she rely on the imperfect words from her imperfect mind going into the imperfect ears of another and being, filtered into the imperfect mind of that other?

It is madness. A nightmare. The worst system to ever have been created.

Why couldn't August simply read their mind? See the crafted, gentle, warm, words they have ready for her?

Why does Celeste have to hope she can one day, hopefully, if the stars align, and her mother hasn't been particularly horrible that morning, that she could take what she feels, thinks, means, and have it be perfectly spoken, perfectly heard, perfectly understood?

Absolutely. Completely. Without limitation.

Why must it be so hard to own up to hurt? To resolve their mistakes? To get back what they lost?

This must be one of those things old people talk about.

That Celeste'll understand when she's older, things will be easier as she grows up, so much more will make sense one day.

But what are they supposed to do now? With these huge regrets and these heavy emotions? Why do the old people never say anything about that?

Maybe those people are right, and it *will* be easier when she's older. But Celeste is here right now.

And they need it to be easier right now. While they can still hope to fix it.

Instead of simply sitting in such deep loneliness. Such suffocating isolation. No lover could be bearable, if she still had a best friend.

But no, they had to go for the double whammy, they had to ruin two good things. And get Hathor involved.

Celeste really can't do anything right. And everyone knows, if someone can't be perfect, they don't get anything good. Ever.

'That's how the world works, kid. Get used to it.'

4:38pm 11th March 2011

Dichotomy

"...hey..." Celeste says weakly, waving awkwardly in their uniform, white polo and bottle green skirt.

August's smile dropping, barely believing Celeste would show their face here, let alone unannounced.

The rage boiling, jaw tensing, staring daggers.

"...so... c-can we... t-talk?" Celeste stutters, the question absolutely not escaping unscathed. "P-please...?"

Breathe in. Count to five. This can be done.

"This isn't ok, Celeste." August states, tone measured and calm, stern, bistre eyes meeting skittish cerulean.

The full name hitting Celeste where she's already hurting, but she knows this isn't about her pain, not here and not now.

"I-I know that... I should've tried to... m-message or something..." Celeste replies, small and collapsing, avoiding eye contact like it's their job. "B-but I j-just have something quick, th-that... I think if... I can... j-just... p-please..."

August looks over Celeste, imagining pushing them into the silver banksia, delighting in watching them get covered in the tiny spikes, and scrambling to get up with any grace. But instead, considering a small mercy, and a bargaining chip.

"This is what I will allow: you say your thing, I say my thing, and you go home." August outlines, picturing the slouching Celeste covered in those banksia spikes. "What do you say?"

Celeste looking up, tiny and woeful, arms low, one hand gripping a wrist, tight and painful.

A vigorous nod. A quick glance. Regretful eyebrows. Tragic.

But not enough for August's rage to subside.

"O-ok... I, um... I know that I-I fucked up..." Celeste begins, trying her best to look August in the eye as much as possible. "I absolutely fucked up. And... I d-did that because I'm a coward who d-didn't know how to be in a... relationship, like, romantically..."

Celeste trailing off. August's anger hot and thick.

"Is that... all you have to say?" She interrogates, pushing words through gritted teeth.

"No! N-no. Also, that... my like, lack of experience is no excuse..." Celeste continues, hands wringing, eyeline low, shoulders high. "B-but if you could... possibly, like, g-give me the chance to make it right... I'd love to have you back as a friend... one d-day."

"...ok."

"Okay?!" Celeste pipes up, ready to jump into August's arms.

"No!" August asserts, holding a hand up. "Not 'ok' like 'that's ok', but 'ok' like 'I hear you and now I'm gonna say my thing, as agreed', ok?"

Celeste deflating instantly, the words cutting through their skin, veins, and flesh, right to the bone, affirming every negative voice in an instant.

But they deserve it. So, who fucking cares?

"You really hurt my fucking feelings." August begins, relaxing into it, words coming easy and free. "I trusted that you weren't ready, and even though I worried it might be because you don't find me hot, I dealt with that on my own-"

"G... I'm sorry I had no idea." Celeste cuts in, defensive and reactionary.

"No. You don't get to interrupt me." August asserts, calm and matter-of-fact. "You agreed, you don't get to disrespect me again."

She's right. No one's ever been more right. And it drives another knife into Celeste's stomach, lacerating the tender flesh, adding to the collection.

Celeste nods. Silent and retreating.

"Ok." August breathes, exhaling the rage, continuing evenly. "This was the wrong thing to do." Her calmness wavering as tears urge their way out.

She takes a moment, clearing her throat, wiping her nose swiftly.

"It's not just wrong because you went and... felt comfortable enough with Hathor right away, though that is fucked up." August explains, composed and clear, bubbling with heavy emotions underneath. "But because... you never came to me and talked about this. It could've been uncomfortable with me." She takes in a breath, fast and vicious, helping the screaming fury stay at bay. "You betrayed my trust, instead of just coming to me and being honest. And... fuck you for that."

Celeste looking up, the final words shocking them enough to brave August's gaze.

It's vicious and loaded, speaking of twisted tears and harrowing anger, a scar deep where no one can see.

She closes the screen door, locking it purposefully.

Celeste left holding the wooden door, alone under the veranda. A festive ornament of a person, just for decoration.

"Now get in your fancy fucking car." August instructs, neck tensing, jaw once again tight. "And make sure you do better with the next person."

The words have barely left her rose lips, and August is walking away, barrier already established, and highlighted as Celeste watches her go.

August hears the wooden door gently close from the corridor, waiting with a hand over her mouth, for the sound of a car door opening and closing.

Gripping her cheeks, fingers digging into the soft skin, nose breathing hot over her hand, and mercifully, she hears the distinct clunk-pause-clunk.

She's sliding down the wall before her mind realises she's moving.

Knees weak, legs spent, shoulders aching. Hand coming down, salt flowing freely, wails escaping into the house, echoing along the corridor, the misery cacophony.

Wailing becoming screams. Screaming becoming punches. Punching becoming collapse.

Knuckles scuffed from the carpet. Face leaking and red. Body heaving and alone.

Celeste has burrowed steadily, insidiously, into her system, and letting go wasn't a linear journey.

But knowing and applying are two different things. She can know the grief, confusion, and raw fury is going to come in waves, and still be surprised when it does.

She's only human. She's only got one heart. And she's still trying to pick up every last shard, let alone starting to glue it back together.

"Kære!" Alf calls, hearing the sobs from the front door. "Er det dig?"

"Ja!" August calls back, voice ravaged and unsteady. "...det er mig."

Alf rushing to her side, lifting her head into his lap, tracing soft fingers through her short, dark, ringlet curls.

"You want to talk, kære?" Alf asks, voice low and comforting. "Or you want to sit quiet?"

"It's Celeste..." She answers, voice lacerating every cell along the way, painful, but nothing she hasn't handled before. "They fucking... came here and, like... I don't even know... they were just a shit..."

"Oh, kære." Alf soothes, folding over, placing temple to temple, moving their hand to squeeze her arm, covering her like a blanket. "That sounds awful, I'm so sorry."

"Me too…" August replies, words choked with tears, voice rough and scratching. "I thought I was over the whole thing… but they like, showed up and I was so angry… like I was just after they told me."

"That's ok, kære, anger is natural." Alf soothes, voice surrounding August, reverberating all around her body. "Anger tells us when-"

"-something isn't right." August finishes, knowing the words too well, but appreciating hearing them now.

"Exactly, kære… Nothing to fear. Natural. Det er ingenting."

"Ja." August agrees, legs curling up, suddenly cold. "Ingenting."

"Er du kold, kære?" Alf asks, clocking August's movement.

"Nej, jeg fint." August lies, surrounding her legs with arms, both bare in her Summer uniform.

"Du er ikke fint, kære." Alf pushes back gently, watching their daughter continue to curl up. "Come, we run you a bath, we warm you up. Come now."

Alf doesn't wait for an answer, unfolding himself slowly, and easing August to her feet, her legs wobbling, almost buckling on the way up.

Hooking an arm under her armpit, Alf steadies August, guiding her to the bathroom, and propping her up, with a reassuring gentle arm-rub for good measure, then turning to rinse down the bath, and back for a quick knee-squeeze, before getting the bath running.

"Elsker dig." Alf assures, following their words with a forehead kiss, short whiskers a little scratchy, and always comforting. "Which one you want?"

Routing around in the cabinet, Alf lists off a number of oils, washes, and bath bomb labels, finally lifting his head when August gives a 'mmm' to Rosewood & Geranium body wash.

Alf making a dorky display of showing the bottle like they're a waiter presenting wine at a restaurant.

"Is this to your liking, mademoiselle?" Alf asks, adding a final flourish and a smile.

"Yes!" August chuckles, wiping her nose on her hand. "Thanks, dad."

"Of course, kære. It's what I'm here to do." Alf replies, pouring a generous amount, and turning to August, bobbing down, holding her tear-and-mucus-covered hand. "I'm here for you always. Always, ok?"

"O-ok..." August cries, tears layering, following well-fell paths.

Alf bobs up, grabbing a few tissues, handing them wordlessly to August, and bobbing back down.

"You are my world, kære." Alf states, easy and loving. "Elsker dig happy, Elsker dig sad, Elsker dig with every breath I take into my body. And, I always be here for you."

"Og... j-jeg Elsker dig." August replies, trying to wipe half-dried tears and fresh ones alike, as her voice shakes under the weight of unconditional love.

Alf watching, smiling up at their daughter, calm hands on knees, hoping only to ground her, be present here with her, communicate the oceans they would swim to simply be by her side.

August crying and drying, nodding silently, knowing she is safe here, in any room of this house, in any state, to ask any question, to voice any thought.

Nothing more treasured than a soft place to land.

11:52am 19th January 2011

Dear Celeste

If I could write, I'd write you a novel, but you'd never read it.

If I could sing, I'd sing you an opera, but you wouldn't listen.

If I could shoot, I'd photograph you every day, but you'd never look over them, too afraid of that much love.

I wish you could see yourself like I see you.

I wish you could see how I hurt for you.

I wish you could see us as I imagined us, celebrating every win, standing proud on the podium of deep affection.

Under your spell I fell.

Under your spell I stayed.

Under the night sky I cried, until my eyes rolled out of head, smashing on the cold tile.

How I worshipped you.

How I always hoped to please you.

How I stumbled, with a spike through my heart, coughing up blood on the flowers I planted for you.

Opening my heart to you.

Opening my mind to our memories.

Opening my books to words of you, writing letters to no one, scattering hopes on the wings of infinity.

6:27pm 30th June 2010

So, This Is… My… Girlfriend.

I Guess?

"Hesi, Tickle! Wakadii hako?" Faye calls, voice carrying through a cloud of Millie Small, and down the corridor.

"Taswera maswerawo, Mum!" August calls back, clear enough to carry all the way into the kitchen, taking off her forest green bomber jacket, and bringing it to a hook. "Celeste is with me!"

Stopping in their tracks, Mackintosh beige cotton field jacket in hand, Celeste anxiously leans closer to August, suddenly stiff and hurried.

"Did you… did you ask her if that was ok?" Celeste whispers, energy changing in a moment, exuding thick worry. "What if it's not?"

August need not answer, as Faye jumps in first.

"Hesi, Celeste! Wonderful to have you! Make sure you both take off your shoes!"

The warm welcome can only subside Celeste's worry so much. As quick and hateful, a thousand voices echo around their mind, proclaiming they are intruding, that they're downright unwelcome, and Faye's words are that worst of offenses: Stone. Cold. Lies.

But Celeste is already here, and it'd be even worse to just leave, surely.

Wandering through a smog of self-critique, Celeste makes her way to the kitchen, passing tribal masks and fauvist paintings, beaded artworks and modern needlepoints, the comfort and beauty of August's home lost on her.

Eyes blank, limbs unfeeling, head storming with vitriol, walking in August's wake like a child, following their parent around a birthday party.

Celeste's shift unnoticed by August, as she bounds toward the reggae and scent of onions frying in jerk seasoning, brimming with news for her mother.

"How was the film, Tickle?" Faye asks, as the pair round the kitchen arch, standing in the threshold for a pause.

Celeste hanging back, August walking up to her mother, waiting with arms open. Faye taking her daughter into a tight hug, the sight still foreign to Celeste, despite witnessing it so many times before, over so many years.

August burying herself in the comforting, soft teal of her mother's merino wool cardigan, temple to cheek, wrapping arms around her citrus-patterned apron, feeling at home truly and completely.

"It was good. There was hardly anyone there, which was... cool." She replies, shifting in her mother's embrace to face Celeste, and raising her eyebrows.

August's hand on the armrest flashes in Celeste's mind. Fingers intertwining, eyes locking in the dark, a kiss electric and powerful, tingles and fireworks in the back of Metro 5.

Like flying through space, like diving into sweet syrup, like being anywhere but this small town. What a torturous relief.

"Manheru Celeste! Did you like the film too?" Faye asks, turning in her spot by the stove, yanking Celeste from the images playing behind empty cerulean eyes.

August drying her hands, easily falling into Helper Mode in a kitchen so familiar, flinging a now-damp lemon-printed tea towel over her shoulder, and busying herself with peeling freshly washed potatoes. Unable to see Celeste's stiffness for what it is.

Celeste watching with simmering jealousy rushing through their system. As though August's time with her mother is cherished and beautiful, something to be enjoyed.

Faye smiling at an adrift Celeste, awaiting a reply, but mostly a chance to check in with such a shaky soul.

"Manheru Dr. Tandi, um... ye-yeah... it was good." Celeste hastily replies, feeling far too perceived by Faye's warm gaze, even from across the kitchen. "Thank you for... for asking."

"Of course, Celeste!" Faye follows up, genuine and loving, busying herself with opening several cans of beans, then checking on the onions slowly sauteing. "And you're staying for dinner?"

Celeste wringing her hands in response, eyes low, short mousy locks falling forward, covering a pale, cowering face.

"Yeah! That's ok, right?" August jumps in, popping up, holding a large pot, and plopping the potatoes in.

"I'd love to have you stay for dinner." Faye replies, leaving the frying onions, closing the small distance, and facing a nervous Celeste. "Would you like to call your parents, and let them know?"

Celeste meets Faye's warm eyes.

Deep, liquorice pools of absolute kindness, shallow crow's feet only visible when she smiles this caring and wide, pushing up warm, dark, full cheeks. Fond and tender.

Looking at Celeste as though they actually matter, as though they are a whole person, and their comfort is important.

Here, in a house that isn't even their home.

A dull pang. In the rotting, harrowing, pit, where Celeste keeps her anger, telling her so much of her pain could've been avoided, if only Faye could've been her mother, instead of the shell that is Lydia Breadseed.

"Yeah, I'll text Mum now." They reply, coming back to their body, knowing Faye is waiting for answer. "I'm sorry to put you out like this."

"Oh please!" Faye reassures, hand on Celeste's upper arm, giving a light squeeze. "You're welcome any time." And leaning in extra close, she adds: "And maybe some time we can talk about saying 'thank you' instead of 'I'm sorry', but for now, text your Mum."

Faye steps back to the stove, August updating her on the potatoes, and Celeste taking in the sight of equals;

jealousy pulsing through them, as they compose a text to their shadow of a mother.

August keenly recounting the movie she and Celeste just saw, speaking of action sequences, and how Nicholas Cage was 'actually quite good'. Wanting only to fill her mother in, informing of anything she got up to, no matter how ordinary, while out and about this evening.

Faye, enthralled as always, tipping beans into the pan absentmindedly, as her daughter emotes and regales, having the distinct pleasure of soaking in such beautiful energy.

"...and we have news!" August announces, gesturing to Celeste. "Would you like to share it, or I can?"

The words shaking Celeste from their focus. And, pressing send, they're unable to reach any of their own, having completely forgotten what they and August had discussed in the car ride.

Self-loathing is one hell of a drug. Clouding and all-encompassing, sucking the joy from blessed moments.

Bursting with anticipation, August can't see Celeste's vacancy, too absorbed in eagerly glancing between Celeste and her mother, ready to spill her own beans. Knowing there's no one else in the world she'd rather share this update with, except maybe Alf, but they'll be next.

Celeste feeling the swamp of haunting voices drown her, in its shallow, dirty water, robbing her of the present.

It's only August, with excited, bistre eyes, bobbing on the balls of her feet, smile frolicking on her lips, waiting and hoping. And Faye, turning down the burner's heat, shifting loving and complete focus to her daughter, and best friend.

"You can share…" Celeste answers, smile false, words empty.

"Ok!" August bounces, gesturing for Celeste to stand by her side.

They move, reluctant yet trying, baring teeth and concealing emotions, standing next to August, like a player in someone else's show once again.

"Well… Celeste and I are…" August continues, taking Celeste's hand in hers. "Girlfriends!"

How she's beaming, some of it rubbing off on Celeste, trying against every instinct to be present and open.

"That's wonderful!" Faye proclaims, hands clasping, joy radiating. "How about a group hug?"

August nods, excitement seeping into Celeste through palms, as they mirror her nodding, albeit with significantly less fervour.

Faye taking the pair into a fierce hug, saving and poetic, warm like blankets in the deepest winter. Familiar and expected to August, but moreish and incredibly needed for Celeste.

"But oh!" Faye begins, pulling back enough to look at Celeste. "Are you ok with the term 'girlfriends'?"

"Yeah!" Celeste beams, feeling so considered and appreciated, within such a simple gesture. "It doesn't…

you know, feel like, invalidating of my gender, or whatever."

"Ok. Well, you let me know if that changes. And Tickle…" Faye begins, focus turning to August. "You check in about that, ok?"

"Of course, Mum!" She chuckles, like it's easy to be considerate, and reply to your mother, like it's not mental gymnastics, just a simple string of sounds. "You think I don't ask my own girlfriend if they're ok with a gendered term? Come on!"

"…Alriiight…" Faye replies, with playful apprehension, looking to Celeste, and giving a wink. "Gotta keep you in check, Tickle!"

Faye and August's laughter swarming around the three, Celeste freezing where she's standing, unable to process that keeping a teenager in check is so foreign in this house, it warrants laughter.

Feeling instead like the fool in the Globe Theatre, gangly and pathetic, as everyone howls with laughter, from the pit to the upper gallery, as they jingle around on stage for the enjoyment of others.

"Well, I'm glad you're with someone you know so well, Tickle." Faye continues, chuckles subsiding. "And Celeste, you've got a good one here." She concludes, winking again.

Celeste manages an ingenuine smile in response, appreciating the sentiment, but disoriented as usual, by the still-foreign mother-child dynamic that is Faye and August.

August seeing Celeste's half-smile and knowing that's just how they are sometimes, the British repression thick and entrenched, but always insisting August not worry about them, asserting it makes them feel spotlit and awkward.

Instead, she feels the joy swarm her, looking from Celeste to her mother, appreciating the beauty of having two people who love her in her arms. The gentle bubble of the potatoes, mixing with the elastic bass, staccato keys, and offbeat drums, of Millie Smalls' Time Will Tell, circling around the warm kitchen, as it wafts from the white and blue CD player.

The open windows fogging with condensation, the Winter air wafting in occasionally, relieving the building heat, as the jerk spices become fragrant, and the potatoes approach a rolling boil, layering, a fever pitch within reach.

But it can wait for now.

Celeste feeling two sets of dark eyes on them, trying their best to smile and seem happy, not just for August and Faye, but for their own sake.

The doubts already creeping in.

Maybe this isn't a good step, maybe she doesn't like August in the romantic sense, maybe these two are better as friends. Or maybe the voices are being horrid again.

Nonetheless, as August and Faye bring in one final squeeze, and return their attention to the stove, projected pictures of times gone by flash in Celeste's mind's eye: joking about the gross boys at school, talking and laughing late into the night, dressing up and doing their best runway walks down that eclectic corridor.

Just kids, making memories together.

Surely, this will be like that, but better. The voices can't be right about this, because then they'd be right about everything.

12:19pm 11th January 2011

The Great

Queer Friend Date

Of 2011

"What did you get?" August asks Hathor, walking out into the high sun of midday, donning her Ray Ban-style, black and chartreuse sunglasses. "Looks good!"

"It is!" Hathor praises, taking a lick, squinting in the brightness. "It's Sofala Gold, obviously. Had to get the star of the show!"

"Of course, the total diva." August jokes along, giving a slight nudge to Hathor. "I got the Caramel Choc Chip."

"Is it a total diva?" Hathor volleys, pulling her magenta, leopard print, aviators from her tee's collar, and fighting her dark waves to put them on. "Does it schedule meetings at nine a.m., and show up at four in the afternoon?"

"It does!" August squawks, barely getting the words out, before laughter taking over, bursting out onto the road.

The trio crossing to King's Park. Settling in among the lush grass, under massive shady trees, surrounded by war memorials and statues, myrtle green wooden benches, vibrant seasonal flowers, and of course, the carillon, sitting smack bang in the centre. All encased in parked cars, pedestrians, and local business, the lively centre of this regional city.

Hathor and August cackling about ice creams, and divas of music and film, Celeste following along in silence, crashing and burning in their effort to not seem completely miserable.

"And what about yours?" Hathor asks, noticing Celeste falling back, and hoping to include them. "Looks good."

"Yeah, it's Choc Hazelnut." Celeste states simply, flashing a false, closed-mouth smile.

"Which you love, don't you?" August tries, nodding with encouragement, hoping to get more words out of The Stone themself. "You get it all the time."

"Yeah." They answer, dry and simple, pushing their pink-tinted, gold-framed sunnies up. "All the time."

"Cool." Hathor attempts, feeling caught between the couple. "It's a good choice."

The reply she receives is a half-smile and a shrug, as Celeste makes another failed effort to hide how misery loves them.

A brief tension wafts in, under the shielding leaves of large, dense, trees, in a frozen moment with frozen cream.

"So, Hathor, you've never been to Annie's before?" August mercifully asks, silently speculating Celeste could be purposely sabotaging this friend-date to keep her all to themself. "We're glad to help you pop your cherry!"

"But I didn't get the cherry, remember?" Hathor joshes, tilting her head, and furrowing dark brows playfully, for a little extra pizzaz.

"That's right!" August laughs, covering her mouth, not wanting to spit any choc chips. "You did say no to the cherry!"

More cackling, a genuine bond forming in seconds. Something Hathor has been craving for so long: a chance to connect with her peers.

"And what do you two usually do?" Hathor asks, curious about young queer love, and feeling bold enough, surrounded by sun and laughter. "Like, when youse go on dates?"

"Oh. Loads of stuff." August answers, smiling at Celeste, hoping for a little energy. "Don't we? Like, go to the movies, sleepovers, just hang out and talk. Right?"

"Yeah... totally." Celeste manages, flashing another closed-mouth false grin, convincing no one.

"And you could always join us!" August tries to save, hoping that being double-enthused will make up for Celeste's reservations. "Or we could try something you like!"

"I mean, that all sounds great to me." Hathor beams, taking another lick of her ice cream. "Anything other than doing nothing at home is like, exactly what I wanna do."

"I hear that." Celeste pipes up, the smallest amount of actual interest in their tone.

A silent shared glance between August and Hathor, as Celeste takes a lick of her Choc Hazelnut, watching some small kids chase each other around.

"Maybe we should do that." They remark, dry as sand, intention unclear.

"...maybe we should... finish our ice creams first." August responds, trying to inject more humour into her reply.

"Otherwise, it might get messy!" Hathor volleys, crunching into her waffle cone.

"That could be fun." Celeste replies, tone once again unclear. "A little mess couldn't hurt."

"Cheers to that!" Hathor jokes, lifting her remaining cone.

August busting out into hearty laughter, Hathor joining, Celeste looking to the kids again.

Thinking of when they were smaller, running around with August, yelling into the sky, legs giving out, falling to the grass, collapsing in each other's arms.

How things change, and keep changing. Celeste knowing the jealousy is taking over, and willing it back down, but falling short every time.

Seeing August slip through her fingers, knowing she's coming off as odd, harsh, unfriendly, but being unable to stop, let alone speak her anxieties out into the afternoon.

Instead, enviously watching Hathor, as she connects with August, on a level they never managed to.

So they just sit, in the shade of the beating sun, retreating, only replying with the occasional single word, until the time comes for everyone to go home. Not that home is ever a place they want to be.

8:17pm 24th January 2011

Just Break My Heart And Go

"So that's it, then?" Hathor asks, voice laced with the tears she's willing to stay inside, as the bricks dig into her grape leggings. "you're just... done with me?"

"It's not like that, Hath." Celeste implores, hands twisting and writhing in her lap, their heart beating furiously. "It's not... it's just not like that."

"What's it like, Cel, please tell me." Hathor begs, wiping a stray tear as soon as it surfaces, determined to not bawl her eyes out, not in front of anyone, ever.

Celeste sits in the pointed silence, the echo of the summer ringing in their ears, eclipsed in a moment by the nonchalant, glib, wave of her mother, as her cruel words take over, swirling around their head.

'Have your little moment, but don't pretend to yourself you're going to end up with some girl, you're just not'.

You're just not.

Over and over it reverberates. Bouncing and amplifying. Strong enough to shatter hearts.

This is how it has to be.

"It was a passing thing, it's over." Celeste mumbles, hands now busy with the draw string of her hunter green linen shorts.

The words float over to Hathor, crawling into her ears, scraping at the walls of her skull, burrowing down into her stomach, and piercing the lining, acid leaking out into her abdomen, burning through her body, ravaging her insides, like nothing she's ever known.

Venom. Bile. Horror.

And those tears she's trying so hard to hold back, flowing like a poisoned river, down her hot cheeks, to her chin, and falling down, to her baby blue Vans, cemented into the ground.

She is frozen. Already shattered. Unable to pick herself up. Not yet.

'...it's a passing thing...'

It stings deep down in Hathor's soul. She wants to scream. To hit something. To get the fuck out of here.

But she can't. She is ravaged by pain, tears spilling into the daylit evening, body rooted to the ground.

"Please say something." Celeste implores, the pale skin on their hands red underneath, the winding of the drawstring around their fingers taking its toll so fiercely. "Please, Hath."

Hathor can feel her voice catch in her throat, her body unable to respond. Too swamped to form words.

"Hath..."

Celeste's voice is desperate, small, hurting, but she doesn't know how to make it better, what to do, what to say, she just knows this has to be over. It just has to be done.

"Hath, please..."

A rigid Hathor manages to start shaking her head, her chest heaving with the breath of the revived, as her thick brow furrows and russet her eyes close. Slowly returning to her body, coming back to the moment.

"What do you- what do you want me to say? This hurts so much, I don't want to be here." Hathor speaks, her words thick with strain, her voice low and scratchy. "Is that what you want me to say?"

"Of course not. I don't- there's not- Hath-"

"Fuck off, Cel!" Hathor yells, pulling her hand back as Celeste reaches to take it. "Fuck... off... I'll fucking- I'll see you at school. And I won't- I won't fucking say anything."

A promise. A threat. A challenge.

Hathor's words hit Celeste like freezing water to the face. Harsh, disorientating, forceful. Sinking into their skin, twisting its way into their system, imprinting into their bloodstream.

A tattoo of a truly misguided moment, created by a scared and flawed teenager.

Those words might be called-for, even understandable, but that doesn't mean they don't burn.

Celeste knew school next month would be hell either way.

But it shouldn't be. Because she shouldn't even care. This was nothing. A blip in her life. She'll grow up and get over it.

So right now, they'll just stay. Watching Hathor storming off, among the delayed afternoon, under the beaming cyan sky, completely exposed to anyone's prying small country town eyes.

And there's nothing she can do. This is her own shortcoming, and she knows it. So, let's sit on the scratching red brick retaining wall about it.

At least for a little while.

10:48pm 24th January 2011

It's Only Twelve More Months,

I Can Do It

What cruel torture, to finally taste deliverance, and have it so swiftly pulled away.

The sweetest dream, and she's been rudely awoken.

Laying on her bedroom floor with her haunts and her tears, Hathor watches the teak fan spin, replaying Celeste dumping her just two hours ago.

How she wandered a few streets down, and hurried into the Metro 5, stowing away in the toilets to cry, not knowing if it'd be safe to come home in tears.

To emerge into the inky black of the January evening, the night finally come, and knowing it must be late, only to run home, and find it empty, having forgotten her parents went to Sydney today, and wouldn't be home until midnight.

What deeply funny pain, to have been able to come back to a vacant house to cry, only to have avoided it, because a public toilet at the cinema, was guaranteed to be more emotionally secure.

And what tragically hilarious irony, to have the house to herself, as a teenager, with almost no other chances to be deviant, only to have no one to sin with tonight.

She'll have to hang onto that one fumbling, exciting, thrilling experience for dear life. It will have to be enough for her, a snapshot of lust, of teenage desire, an explicit kiss in the dark, a touch in the hidden moments of time.

She'll have to take it, it'll have to tide her over, and one day, not soon enough, she'll have the chance for more.

There'll be cheek kisses in the daylight, laughs in the park on a Sunday, hugs in the coffee shop.

But for now, for here, for her, just one moment will have to do.

The hope for more, it'll have to keep her strong, keep her going.

The enchanted youthful love story wasn't hers to know, as it often isn't for those like her.

Hathor balls herself up, tucking knees into her chest, arms gripping tightly around, hugging and pressing.

"Twelve more months..." she whispers, silent salt streaming. "Only twelve more months."

Tighter and tighter. Over and over. A broken record of self-soothing.

All she has to do is get through this final school year, and she's out, she's gone. A ghost to her parents, and to this shitstain of a town. Neither want her as she is anyway.

And soon enough, that won't even matter. She can sense it, taste it, so close, so near.

She just has to be strong right now, and it'll pass, it has to.

Twelve. More. Months.

She can do it.

7:28pm 13th January 2021

Who's That?

A click. Another click. Hundreds of photos.

Hathor had intended to just find one, but now she's spoilt for choice.

"Who's that?" Freddie asks, leaning in, chin on Hathor's shoulder, palm on the other side.

"Oh... that's Celeste." Hathor answers, staring through the image.

Celeste and Hathor, on a storied night in 2011, lit by the Olympus camera's flash, a kiss on the cheek, a smile on the other's lips. The background swallowed by the flash's brightness.

But Hathor knows exactly where it was.

Her russet eyes unfocusing, the moment swarming her, sticky and gooey, a memory made of syrup, she's right back there.

Celeste's camera gone off, the scene clear.

The two in the cinema on a school holiday Friday, credits rolling, empty popcorn in laps, scratchy seats sinking into thinly-covered legs, two teenagers at the back of the movies, taking a photo in the dark for novelty and prosperity.

And out they both headed, to Celeste's car, where they shared a first.

It was clumsy, sweaty, urgent.

But it was special, a moment of 'yes', among a chorus of 'no'.

Hathor can taste the balmy night air, mouth cold from the slushie, the taste of frozen berry on her lips, as she throws the empty cup in the bin.

The sun only just set at ten p.m., deepest violet painted all over the sky, a tiny glint of saffron still hanging on for dear life, as the night comes into full force, pushing the sun into the horizon.

"Who's Celeste?" Freddie asks, running her hand down to Hathor's lower back, tracing gentle touches.

"They're, um… like, um…" Hathor scrambles, coming back to the present. "They're an old friend." She manages, half-truth, half-lie.

"They look happy in the photo… so do you." Freddie muses, landing a lazy kiss on Hathor's shoulder. "And wow, do you look young!"

"Y-yeah…" Hathor stutters, mind busy. "It's um… weird to, um… yeah."

"And were those ones at your Grad?" Freddie asks, noting Hathor changing, and wanting to give her a chance to move away from this subject. "You look so dressed up!"

Hathor mumbles an 'oh yeah', scrolling down to the snapshots of her graduation formal, opening up them up in Photos, for Freddie to click through, and make passing observations about, while Hathor barely manages more than one-word responses.

She's adrift in something painful and universal. A snapshot of youth and desire that will never be again.

An urgency, a speed, a flash of lightening in a thunderstorm.

"Are you ok, Thor?" Freddie asks, noting Hathor's change sticking like sugar in the sun. "You seem far away."

"Yeah, I guess not, aye." Hathor admits, feeling the truth of Freddie's words.

"Anything I can do?" Freddie asks, moving around to Hathor's side, bobbing down, always trying to make herself smaller, living in such a tall frame.

"I don't know..." Hathor replies, smiling weakly. "Maybe no more pictures for now."

"Yeah, of course." Freddie agrees, placing her palms gently on Hathor's knees, grounding them both.

"Yeah, it's just... a bit... weird." Hathor stumbles, such hollowness overtaking her, ripping right through, a shot to the chest.

Tiny tears forming at the very corners.

"Oh, I'm getting..." Hathor sniffles, trying to sprinkle some humour into her words, dabbing at the pooling water. "Oh, ok."

"Yeah, it's ok." Freddie states, matter-of-fact as you like, as though nothing could shake her from Hathor's side. "Hug?"

Hathor standing up from the lavender desk chair, Freddie following, both slightly unsteady, Hathor leaning into waiting arms. Her fingers splaying out onto shoulder blades, sinking into Freddie's loose, hot pink cotton.

"You wanna talk about it?" Freddie asks into Hathor's dark waves, grasping onto a shaky lower back, tracing circles on faded, plum, rayon. "Or we can stay quiet."

Hathor gripping tighter, shuffling knees closer, thighs pressing, tummies together, hearts so close, burying her head into Freddie's neck.

"I don't know." Hathor replies, muffled and small. "This is nice, but."

"It is nice." Freddie assures, continuing her circles. "And here I was thinking seeing myself in my Grad suit would be the big emotional moment."

Hathor laughs softly, shrouded in pain, but rippling out all the same.

"To be fair, closeted Freddie was giving pussy." Hathor jokes back, words scraping her tear-ravaged throat on the way out.

"Oh, you spoil me." Freddie volleys, smiling into Hathor's hair. "I wish I could've served pussy, I was too busy being a *sensitive* boy."

"Well you're succeeding at being a sensitive woman right now, does that count?" Hathor jokes, lifting her chin to rest on Freddie's shoulder.

"Yeah, I'll take it." Freddie laughs, a lock of Hathor's dark waves kicking up. "Tell me to fuck off, but I'm guessing Celeste was more than a friend."

"They were, you don't have to fuck off, but." Hathor answers, her head bobbing awkwardly in the tight embrace, pushing up from the jaw as her words form. "And they were less too."

"Got it."

10:57pm 14th January 2011

I've Never Been Absolutely

Famished Like This

Hot breath, thick air, fogged windows.

Hard kisses, busy hands, discarded clothes.

Hathor's words in Celeste's ear, asking a question she hoped would have a 'yes' answer, and in turn, travelling kisses to Celeste's décolletage when she received that 'yes', lips kissing as fast fingers pull at sports bra straps.

Celeste calling out curses, moaning affirmations, pulling off their knickers, sinking fingertips into Hathor's neck, shoulders, and arms.

Hathor travelling down further, Celeste's skin tasting of sweat, feeling like heaven, smelling of Chance Eau Fraîche, the fresh citrus scent filling the small vehicle, as the heat inside builds and intensifies, layering steam all around two vibrant souls, in the cover of night.

"Please, please, please..." Celeste murmurs out, consumed by arousal, their body shaking under the weight of such sensation. "kiss me there..."

Hathor smiling up at Celeste, unseen in the haze of teenage desire, and the darkness of a car parked behind the cinema.

She licks gently, unsure of how forceful to be, hoping for guidance from Celeste's words, or movements, anything to be the beacon guiding her way.

"Urghhhh... more pleaseeee..." Celeste pleads, absorbed in the collecting pleasure, gone to the moment.

Hathor has the answer. Kissing, licking, swirling, taking in the scents, tastes, and sensations of being between another's thighs. It's beauty, it's salvation, it's comfort.

"Oh yes, urghhh..." Celeste calls out, the all-consuming sensation building, understanding washing over, such cleansing magic. "Yes, yes, right there!"

Celeste is here. Right here. Nothing else is entering, or able to enter her mind. She simply is. Hovering in the inky midnight, entirely connected to the present, nothing able to pull her forward or back.

Clarity.

Gripping Hathor's shoulders, squeezing their thighs around Hathor's cheeks, the wonder surging through their body, what marvellous, divine connection.

Building, layering, almost.

The squeeze taking Hathor's breath away, unexpected yet welcome, wanting to feel more of this, she can't get enough, ravenous and alight. Starving and satiated at the same time, swinging in the space between substantial and supposed, something so shaky yet impossible not to seize.

The rush coming through Celeste, bursting, overcoming their system.

Letting out a low moan, rolling their head back, they call out curses, over and over.

The electricity coursing through her body, like rescue, like escape, like freedom.

Astonishing in its intensity. Breathtaking. Illuminating. Validating.

Hathor watching them, an outline lit by the foggy light of the distant streetlamp, vague shapes barely visible, yet magical and enchanting. A mirage, a chimera, an impression of an idea of a concept. Utterly sublime.

Celeste's breath steadying, their body relaxing, their head rolling back to Hathor, trying to make out rich russet eyes in the darkness, through the thick air: a hazy image of their first time.

Like a photograph kept in a box for decades, colours faded by time, edges ravaged by the elements, yet clear and treasured. Able to be taken out and held to the chest, serving its exquisite purpose: capturing a memory so important, it demands to exist in the physical world.

Intoxicated in the moment, lost in her senses, Celeste materialises back on Earth, reaching for Hathor's face, guiding voracious mouths into a dreamy kiss.

What glory, what beauty, what wondrous blessing, to taste themself on Hathor's tongue, drinking in their own pleasure, the elixir of life.

Both swimming in the air, heavy with punchy citrus, cedar, and jasmine, as Celeste sweats through her perfume. Mixing with deep wooden, leafy, cleansing notes, as Hathor's Forest Fresh roll on evaporates into the steamy thickness.

Messy and rushed, secret and dark, with hands wild. How immeasurably perfect.

Celeste pulling back, chin wet, lips soaked, looking lustfully into Hathor's dark eyes.

"And... you?" They ask, simple and loaded with meaning.

"Yeah?" Hathor responds, filled with desire, unspent energy, and the slightest trace of hesitation.

"Yeah."

It's all Celeste needs.

Shuffling. Fierce and graceless. Urgent and eager.

Until Celeste is over Hathor, taking pause, wanting a chance to take this all in, indulge in this reality, in all its awkward, messy, grandeur.

Leaning in. Kissing hard. Tongues massaging. Worked up and enthusiastic.

Like a hurricane in a slushie cup: powerful, tiny, contained. An uncanny marvel for the ages.

Lips moving, along the jaw, down the neck, along the middle, and over the thin, stretchy, cotton.

Hands following, impatient and wanting.

Hathor reaching, trying to pull off her briefs, fingers shambling, all thumbs and without deftness, until Celeste covers their hands over hers, silently asking.

The reply coming in the form of Hathor retreating slowly, and whispering a 'yes' into the smog of desire.

Briefs flying off, and vivacious fingers tracing along hot skin, kisses tracing thighs and settling somewhere special.

"Argh, yes yes yes!" Hathor calls out, the sudden sensation barrelling through her system, incredible and sacred. "Th-that's good!"

Breathing heavy, hands reaching to the roof, palms pressing into the material and padding, willing herself to embrace the pleasure, as it threatens to overwhelm.

Pure lightening shooting through her capillaries, flooding every tendon with white-hot sensation. Gliding on the wind of pleasure, a bird taking flight for the first time.

Celeste looking up, Hathor nodding, speechless, ignited, drifting in the splendour.

Fingers snapping to thighs, hoping to hold on, mouth busy, kisses erotic, tasting, rapt in her, deific and mesmerising.

Watching in disbelief, only a silhouette, but no meaning lost, what a blessing to make another feel so powerfully.

Shoulders tensing, fingertips digging in, bliss accumulating, heaping, about to explode, a firework in the sky.

"I'm... I-I'm..." Hathor manages, head pressing against the window, body inundated.

Screaming through her system, ravaging and intense, release like no other, monumental and zealous.

Everything fading, soul ascending, seeing through time, floating through the stars, exploring the heavens, astonishing affirmation.

Hands relaxing, shoulders dropping, neck releasing.

Celeste slowing, looking up, chin glistening in the diffused light, absolutely delighted.

"Fuck…" They declare, watching Hathor with reverence, as though she's a deity to be worshipped.

"Yeah." Hathor breathes, thick and loaded, a small chuckle following.

Celeste sitting up, hand on Hathor's calf, cerulean locked on russet.

Windows foggy, air thick, scents swirling around, like swimming through lust.

Hathor sitting up enough to lean in, Celeste closing the gap, lips meeting, glorious and liberating.

Wet and delicious, Hathor tasting herself and Celeste at once, divine union, intertwining in a dark parked car, messy and highly-anticipated.

12:01am 1st January 2011

MFW Shawty Is Absolutely,

Completely,

And Undoubtedly,

Like A Melody

Lips locking, among the fireworks, engulfed in thunderous drum-and-bass, weaving synths, and smooth vocals, charging through the air at Earth-rumbling volume.

The sky alight with colour, whirling and bursting, painting with fire, illuminating the midnight, ringing in another year.

Just two teens, kissing deep and slow, between the noise and lights, hidden and seen, on the dead grass and gravel, in the temperate night.

Celeste pulling back slowly, beaming at the sight of August.

Bistre eyes closed, brown cheeks blushing brilliant raspberry, face serene, full, rose lips slightly pursed, completely spellbound.

Flashes lighting her, seconds at a time, photos being snapped in the black of hard night.

She's wonder, she's magnificence, a regal portrait come to life. And she's enamoured by Celeste. What triumph.

They lean back in, this time to August's ear.

"You're so beautiful!" Celeste praises, loud enough to rip through the roaring music. "It's like, crazy that you're so beautiful!"

August brings a hand up to Celeste's shoulder, running fingertips along the slick, luxurious, ivory, silk.

"No, you!" She deflects, wide smile unnoticed. "But I'll take it!"

"You're like, the most awesome person ever!" Celeste praises, pulling August into her, bodies so close in the chaos. "Ever!"

Fingers caressing the smooth silk, fanning out and sinking into Celeste's soft shoulders, drifting down to the dip in their back, pressing closer, feeling their breasts against hers, laying her chin on their shoulder, swaying back and forth. Inhaling the sublime. Such incredible rescue.

She wasn't sure if this would ever be her reality. But here August is, with her best friend and lover, enjoying the fireworks like it's the easiest thing in the world, romantic and meaningful, simply because it exists.

And what a blessing, to be able to indulge in trivial traditions, just like anyone else. Another ticket holder partaking in the important nonsense.

She doesn't have to be the voice of a generation, or the face of a movement, she can just have special moments, and blend into the crowd, with her girlfriend.

"This is nice." She breathes, unheard in the intensity, lost in the noise.

Celeste continuing the peaceful sway, looking around at the scene, noting all the other couples, and wondering if they see her absolutely crushing it with her love.

It must absolutely kill them all, to see these two, and know none of them could have what Celeste and August have. Never.

What a bunch of jealous, low-life, losers.

With eyes closed, and heart full, August moves to ask a burning question:

"Can I kiss you again?!"

This time her words are heard, eliciting a smirk from Celeste.

A 'yeah' falls from their lips, and they're locking with August's.

No doubt everyone's watching, and they all wish to be Celeste, and what relish, to be the one everyone wants to be.

Soaked in self-assurance, Celeste slides hungry hands down August's back, pulling her in by the arse, fingers sinking into neon orange denim, pressing hips together. Let's see how the crowd likes this one.

August's stomach dropping, trying not to get ahead of herself, to just enjoy this, feeling her body light up, her wanting ignited, head spinning, tingles running rampant in the loud, shining, darkness.

Hands losing grip on Celeste's silk top, hips keening closer, involuntary and elated, sinking further, new and exciting.

Celeste feeling it all, the effect they have in August, like they're magic, like August is beyond thrilled just to be this close to them, as though they possess something inherently incredible.

And in front of all these people? What an absolute rush.

Like the star of her own show, like the biggest deal in this or any city, like she really is special, no matter what words are said at home.

August feeling Celeste pulling away, again, a familiar sensation, but she never wants to push them, or show disappointment too obviously.

Despite herself, a short sigh of frustration leaves her lips, the smallest communication that she wants more, she has for a long time.

And luckily, like so much else, it's drowned out by the bursting fireworks and pounding music, a small save in a contradicting, intense, charged, time.

Celeste moving her hands from neon orange denim, to Maya blue linen, and up to short, dark, ringlet curls, brushing them away from August's flushed face.

"See? Beautiful!" Celeste asserts, shouting over the festivities.

August smiling. Gooey at the words, melting under Celeste's touch. How could she ever think of more, when she receives so much?

This doesn't have to be enough, it already is. Clearly. Otherwise, she wouldn't feel so captivated by Celeste.

There it is. That look of absolute devotion. What an incredible feeling, to make someone as special as August feel so wonderful. The highest trip, the strongest line, a sip right to the brain.

"Maybe we could... talk about..." August tries, absolutely consumed, with just the right balance of courage to bring it up again. "you know... us... having sex..."

Celeste staring at August, like a homeowner scanning the garden maintained by another, enjoying the results, but unaware of the work involved, and unable to hear August's words as they leave rose lips.

Just syllables sunk in the frenzy of New Year's.

"What?!" They shout, inches from August's face, cutting through the noise. "You say something?!"

August feels it. That deep pang. Another affirmation that Celeste isn't ready to open up to her, that she's not doing enough to help them feel comfortable and safe.

"No, nothing!" She lies, turning to watch the fireworks, arm around Celeste.

They smile, turning as well, head on August's shoulder. Excited to tick 'New Years with a girlfriend' off the list.

4:26pm 2nd January 2011

Sugar And Spice

And Everything Awkward

About Kissing My Girlfriend

The calmness and safety of home, the hot midday stumbling into a warm, overcast afternoon, and Celeste, here in the kitchen with her.

August taking two bowls of rich, decadent, chocolate cake, hot to the touch, from the microwave. The icing melting, slipping down the sides, pooling at the bottom of turquoise bowls.

She looks to Celeste, smiling and glancing over, sexuality in bistre eyes, silent communication of hormonal desire.

Celeste lavishing the attention, bathing in the care and love, wanting as much of August's divine attention as she'll bestow upon them.

Closing the gap, August reaches past Celeste, eyes locking, shoulders touching, and producing the icing sugar, brushing back, tantalisingly close.

She turns swiftly, her back to Celeste, taking in a sharp breath, eyes wide, barely believing she was just that smooth, and enjoying the full body reaction.

Heart pounding in her throat, raspberry flush rising in her brown cheeks, stomach dropping, drawing a long, cooling breath through pursed, rose lips.

August retrieves a small sieve from the drawer, turning to Celeste, gaze locking, dunking it into the icing sugar packet, picking up far too much sweetness.

Sliding each bowl over, seamless and smirking, she guides the sieve over, tapping once, twice, three times, four.

The sugar, light as air, cascading down to the deep rich cake, absorbed by the warmth and richness of the chocolate dessert.

It floats down, and disappears – temporary and glorious.

All the while, August looking over Celeste with intense flirtation, moving slow and sensual.

She returns the sieve to the pack, pulling her fingers back, to reveal they're covered in the sugary goodness.

Celeste watching her, unsure of the response August is hoping for, and knowing they're not feeling how they're supposed to. Somewhere, they know this is intended to arouse, but despite August looking inviting, it's not inviting a response from them.

But maybe Celeste just isn't close enough.

With intention, she takes one, two, three steps, and she's hip-to-hip with August, feeling the body heat, and wondering when it's supposed to start feeling good.

August brings her sugary index finger to her own lips, and runs it along the lower lip, leaving the powdery trace behind.

She reaches for Celeste, who goes along with it, leaning in with closed eyes, and feeling August run her ring finger along their thin, peach lips. Bottom, then top.

It's different. Kind of romantic and quirky, like a sweet romcom come to life, and Celeste is feeling it: wanted, desired, she's the one to be wooed.

Alighting their being, the main character in their own story, the one everyone wishes they could be, here with their girlfriend, winning the game.

August watching a serene Celeste, eyes closed, lips sugary sweet, leaning into this moment with her, present, and savouring her touch.

Smiling to herself, she brings a hand up to Celeste's cheek, and their sugary lips to hers.

They're melting into it, opening to August, as she tastes the sweet, inviting presence of an all-speed, no-breaks kiss. Ferocious. Feverish.

Sure, August gets mixed signals from Celeste, but when she kisses them, it's intense, powerful, like Celeste is awoken by only her.

The kiss of life. Resuscitation. Like dragging them out of the water and onto the shore. Hands and mouth bringing them back to life. Under the beating sky. Sand seeping into skin. Holding life in her very hands.

Celeste running a hand around to the back of August's neck, pulling her in closer, deeper. Tongue on tongue, open and passionate. Hoping that going all-in will elicit the intensity that's often missing.

And it's nice, even with no one watching, even with no fanfare, and even without her being the instigator. She still enjoys the sensations, August's body against hers, the sweetness passing back and forth.

Maybe it doesn't always feel like fireworks, and maybe it never will.

But either way, that's enough trying for now.

Celeste pulling back, looking at the cake, hoping for something else to be in their mouth.

August's eyes opening slowly, lost in the now, head spinning, balance uneasy, cheeks flushing raspberry under rich brown tones.

What a wonder, to taste Celeste, to fall into them, to be their girlfriend, and enjoy such gorgeous closeness.

And she did that. August was sexy and seductive, and it worked, she wooed Celeste, and pulled them in for once.

What achievement and what a rush. She's kind of the swaggiest ever.

"How about we go eat these then?" Celeste asks, lifting her bowl, and slipping away from August.

Dreamy, lost, August barely notices the brush-off, trying her best just not to fall right over in her kitchen. Lest it be slightly less swaggy than her previous move.

Celeste isn't waiting for an answer, and makes their way back to the lounge room, hoping to get back to the stack of Video Ezy DVDs waiting on the coffee table, and not think about why they're not feeling the tingle during a kiss with August.

Plopping down on the butterscotch couch, she stares at the stack, waiting for August to join, and get back to something that doesn't involve exchanging saliva.

Without the crowds and the excitement, it's not doing it for them.

So used to performing on a stage, not sure who they are without and audience.

August beaming to herself, sugary fingers dancing on tingling rose lips, feeling electricity running from toes to hips, from shoulders to wrists, from spine to skull, light as a feather, yet charged like an electric fence.

Overjoyed to have such a moment with Celeste, putting back the icing sugar while glowing, alone in the kitchen.

Washing sticky hands in a haze, smile blooming on her lips.

Taking her cake and heading in to join Celeste, excited for another movie and more cuddles, so glad to just soak up more of them, a sponge in the coldest water, without a temperature gauge.

8:16pm 14th January 2011

No, You Don't Get It.

She Like, Literally Insisted.

"Well, she insisted." Celeste clarifies, looking anywhere but Hathor.

"Yeah, no worries." Hathor replies, glancing to the small grassy patch in front of her, wondering just how awkward this movie is going to be. "I'm glad to be out and about, so... yeah."

"Yeah, cool." Celeste responds, looking to the cyan sky with its sparce clouds, glad for the cooler weather. "Like, she insisted, so..."

"Yeah, you said." Hathor nods, burning holes into the grass, too uncomfortable for eye contact. "And, it's all good."

"Yeah, it's just like..." Celeste begins, unsure if they can really say this, but willing it out all the same. "It's not like, I asked her if... you know... it was her idea."

"I... I get that is was August." Hathor states, torn between not wanting to address this, and not being sure if she can handle such tension hanging over the pair for an entire movie.

"Cool. I just wanted you to know it wasn't my idea." Celeste blurts, looking to Hathor finally.

"Oh, you don't wanna hang out with me?" Hathor jokes, looking up to Celeste with a smirk. "Is that right?"

Celeste stumbling, attempting to find two syllables to rub together, let alone articulate.

Causing that smirk to spread wider, Hathor enjoying the tizzy she's sending Celeste into.

"I'm just joking." Hathor says, scrunching up her olive face, shrugging playfully.

"Yeah... yeah, of course." Celeste replies, a little too insistent. "Yeah, that's why I did *my thing*, so..."

"Yeah, totally." Hathor nods, seeing through Celeste as though they're made of glass. "It was a good bit."

Tongue-tied again, Celeste stutters through several sounds, trying to get something out, to no avail.

"That's a good bit too." Hathor continues, biting back a laugh.

"Maybe we should go in." Celeste suggests, gesturing to the Metro 5 behind Hathor. "Get our popcorn and everything."

"Yeah... gotta beat the line." Hathor nods, turning to head inside.

"My treat, by the way." Celeste clarifies, following Hathor. "Not that this is a date, obviously. Like! I-it's a friend-date, obviously, but it wasn't even my idea! A-and it's not, l-like, a date-date! So, like, whatever."

Hathor turning slowly, catching every hurried word as it falls out of Celeste's speeding mouth, word vomit blurting down to her baby blue Vans, sinking into the fabric.

"Yeah..." She replies, biting back a different laugh. "Well, thank you for paying, that's really nice."

"Yeah!" Celeste shouts, realising her volume, and adjusting before continuing. "I mean... yeah. I like to be nice."

"Cool."

Hathor turning again, stifling another laugh, and pausing for a moment at the electric doors, giving them a beat to open.

Celeste walking in her wake, cursing their very existence, but trying to find some solace, in the concept that this night probably couldn't get much worse.

And in some ways, it didn't.

In other ways, it absolutely did.

Two teens sitting up the back of the cinema, watching the beautiful people on the big screen. The darkness giving way to tentative touches, to kisses, and eventually, to the backseat of Celeste's 2008 silver Holden Barina.

A decision that was both a ripple and a catapult. A regret and a cherished memory.

But it was one thing for certain: Celeste's first taste of a high they'd be chasing for years.

3:12pm 12th January 2021

New Regent Street

Ōtautahi (Christchurch)

Aotearoa (New Zealand)

Celeste wringing their hands, falling silent in the crème room, sat on the bistre couch, among the abstract art and muted tones. An accent pillow cursed with consciousness.

Staring at those hands, watching their pale skin become coral, with spots of crimson. The emotions filtering through as best they can.

"I… just- it's like… I just… wish I didn't still get… like this." Celeste finally says, trying to hide their emotions, and hands, between their thighs.

Indigo considers their words for a moment, noting their attempts to hide what was very obvious to her.

"It's not a nice feeling, and I'm very sorry this is happening to you again, it's not ok that they're both ignoring the clear boundary you set." She begins, putting her notes down and leaning in. "And we've discussed it before, but healing isn't linear, knowing that doesn't take away your pain, but it is true."

Celeste begins nodding along, eyes averted, hands tucked, thighs tensing, calves stiffening and bringing knees up. Hoping if they can squeeze tight enough, maybe they can lift off the ground, and fly away from their own life.

"Also, there's so many triggers around this time of year, so it's going to be tough, but that's why I'm here." Indigo continues, smiling softly. "I'm here to help you get through the tough moments, and process them when you're ready, so that eventually, they won't have this hold on you."

Her words easing over to Celeste, soaking into skittish ears, calming a doom-filled soul. Settling, sinking, soothing.

"Mhmm…" Celeste manages, nodding again and remaining tense.

"Do you feel able to talk more about this recent moment?" Indigo enquires, remaining forward, ready to receive Celeste's words.

Celeste grabbing a quick glance to Indigo, noting the waiting warm face, but being unable to hold the eye contact. Sometimes it really hits them just how deeply they aren't ready to take in, let alone, appreciate, any gesture of care.

"Um… yeah… it's just, like… it's the, you know, violation of the boundary, like you said…" Celeste hears their voice break as the words leave their thin, peach lips, tears pouring into syllables, cracking their sounds apart from the inside. "And also, like… this feeling that I'll…"

They pause. Still uneasy in doing so. Always expecting scorn. Especially when they stop for air. Or even worse, start crying. Even after all these years. The scars no one can see. Poisoning their blood to this day.

Indigo reaches for her tissues, extending an arm for Celeste to take the box.

For of course there are no knee-jerk reactions here. Indigo isn't Lydia, nor Timothy, she's not even the perfect, high-achieving, compliant, twins.

Celeste silently taking the box, pulling tissues, drying their eyes, and wiping their nose, before fiddling with the box's corners, hoping to find enough composure in such a futile exercise.

"The... th-the feeling that I'll..." They try, voice soaked in tears, the water splintering through words. "I'll n-never get away from... those two, like, they will al-always have me, like... trapped."

The words are out. Finally. Stated and true. Floating around the crème room like smoke. Wafting about, leaving traces in every inch of the ornate cornices.

If only this room could talk.

"With the way they treated you, that's unfortunately understandable when it comes to abuse." Indigo replies, voice warm and caring, face filled with empathy. "It's not ok that they are both *continuing* to contact you, especially since it's been, what... five years?"

"Yeah." Celeste nods, working their fingers under the flap on the box's side.

"Yes... five years." Indigo nods with heavy regard. "And unfortunately, this is how abusers operate. And it's not ok, it's not respectful, and it's nothing to do with you." Indigo continues, taking in a sharp breath, and exhaling the heaviness.

Fresh tears already begin to fall from Celeste's eyes, their head swimming with threats, assertions, belittling – everything that tried to make them small, unneeding, compliant.

Every time they recall, they're back there. Like no time has passed. Still a scared child. Acting out in any way they can.

"And you're so strong to have gotten away from both of them." Indigo asserts, the words calling Celeste back to the now. "And to continue to stay away, especially considering these recent efforts."

"...Yeah..." Celeste replies, tiny and cracking, fingers pushing through the glue holding the flap to the side of the tissue box. "But it's... it's so big every time."

"What's so big?" Indigo asks, soft and kind.

"Th-the... I don't know..." They try, pushing against the tears, and the engulfing, drowning, everything. "Like, the feeling... it's like I can't escape... I'll never escape."

"I see." Indigo replies, nodding. "And... where do you feel that, where in your body?"

Her words circling Celeste's head, a halo of a question, unable to settle.

"I... don't... I don't know..." Celeste confesses, eyes focusing on their flicking of the cardboard flap, anything to keep their hands busy. "I don't even really know what the feeling... is..."

"Yes, ok." Indigo replies, her tone running deep with empathy. "Would it help for me to list emotions, and you just say, 'yes' or 'no'?"

Celeste considering the question for a beat. Moving to dig fingers under the lower flap on the same side of the box, slow yet ferocious.

"I... th-think I could try..." They stumble, sneaking a quick glance at the patient and caring Indigo, waiting with a compassionate smile and a soft nod. "Um, ok... let's do th-that."

"Ok." Indigo replies, shifting back slightly in her russet armchair, bringing her notes closer. "So... would you say 'anger' fits?"

"I don't... maybe?" Celeste stumbles, brain clambering to calibrate an answer.

"Ok. And where do you usually feel anger in your body?"

"Like... in my... neck?" Celeste suggests, trying to recall the common denominator in their moments of fury.

"That's a hotspot for anger, absolutely." Indigo affirms, noting something down, unseen by a focused Celeste. "Would you say, 'the feeling' is only 'anger'?"

"Um... no?"

"Ok." Indigo nods, making another note, persimmon pen printing away, gentle tone never wavering. "So, would you say that 'sadness' fits?"

"Um..." Celeste repeats, trying to reach for something that keeps dissolving, as they pop the other flap. "I don't know..."

"That's ok." Indigo assures again, ever clear and soft. "What about 'fear', would that fit?"

"I, um..." Celeste tries, new salt falling from their eyes, stinging the lids, travelling paths already laid out on flushed cheeks. "Th-that... um, yes."

"Ok." Indigo nods, making one last jot, and downing her notes for a beat. "And where do you feel 'fear', usually?"

"In... in my..." Celeste searches, low eyes busy, images coming and going in flashes, solution coming through. "Neck, and like... shoulders."

"The same place as 'anger'?" Indigo follows up, bright pen at the ready.

"No... no, I think anger is like... higher." Celeste answers, fingers gesturing as they explain, connecting the dots inside and out. "In my jaw, and my neck a little bit... but like, the fear is like, in my shoulders and chest and like, a little in my neck, that's where they, like meet."

"That makes sense, and you're doing really well right now." Indigo uplifts, nodding and affirming. "This is a big, hard step. You're doing a great job right now.

"Oh, thanks." Celeste responds, caught off-guard as they often are by praise, looking up from their half-undone tissue box. "But like... what is this for?"

"Right, ok... So being able to identify where the feeling is in the body, means that we can identify those feelings in future." Indigo explains, making a quick note as she speaks. "And have plans in place for how to process and move through those feelings."

"So how do I like, process the fear and anger?" Celeste asks, more comfortable in the abstract than the visceral. "Like, what do I do to stop feeling this way?"

"Ok, so, we're not looking to never feel anger and fear." Indigo eases back, asserting, yet full of understanding and care. "We're looking to be able to manage those feelings when they come up."

"Well how do I manage them?" Celeste follows up, frustrated as they often are by the lengthy journey that is healing.

"That's a process in itself." Indigo responds, half-smiling at an impatient Celeste. "And we're making progress."

They can feel it. The flood. Coming in. Through. Out.

"But, it's like... those two spewed this, like, venom into me." They babble, hurt and irritation taking over. "And I'm just so... angry all the time, and I don't want to go back to hooking up, and getting drunk, doing coke, but it's like... I'm always trying to find something wrong with everyone, friends, lovers, whatever, so that I don't have anyone getting close, and it's like, I just want to get venom out. I want to love people, without drugs, without it just being fucking, but I... I can't."

"The fact that you've been able to identify this, and that you have such a desire to work through it, really shows how much progress you've already made." Indigo nods, leaning in, watching a jumpy, reactionary, Celeste.

"But how do I get the venom out?" Celeste presses, voice so little it barely makes it over to Indigo.

"Like this." She soothes, smiling and true. "We talk about the feelings at the core. We learn how to process them. We learn how those feelings are informing your new relationships, and we work to break those patterns."

Celeste hearing the sounds, understanding the sentiment, but still feeling lost and rage-riddled.

"And in the meantime, what do I, like, do?" They ask, voice small, feeling the helplessness engulf, as it often does, any time it pleases. "Just remain alone and like, filled with this, venom? Scared of my fucking parents, dreading Christmas every year?"

"In the meantime, you have me." Indigo reassures, nodding and leaning in far enough to fall forward. "I'm on your side, I'm here to help you in this process. When the memories come back, I'm here to remind you that it wasn't your fault, that it was about them. And I'm here to help you take things slower, give yourself more time and space for processing, until it becomes more familiar."

She watches Celeste, sees their cerulean eyes busy behind low lids, staring through the bowing tissue box, fingers all around it, pressing and releasing with every breath.

"And I just wait for my parents to die?" They question, unable to shake the sensation that this is their only solution.

"What do you hope will happen when they die?" Indigo follows up, sitting back enough to make a sly note.

"I hope to be done with them forever." Celeste confesses, freeing the idea from their haunted mind, eyes blank and body unfeeling. "That they'll like, no longer have this hold on me. That I can move on."

"And do you think you can move on before that?" Indigo queries, watching Celeste's rhythmic, busy hands with empathy and insight.

"...I don't... I don't know." They confess, looking up finally.

Indigo waiting for them, looking into emotionally-exhausted eyes with warm hazel irises, knowing Celeste well enough to make a fair assessment.

"I believe you can."

11:19am 9th January 2011

Fancy Meeting You Here,

In The Indie Rock Section

"Hathor?" August asks, rounding the Movie Soundtracks CD display to greet her classmate. "I thought that was you!"

"Oh, hi August!" Hathor lights up, looking up from her browsing, and pointing to the CD August's holding. "Josie And The Pussycats?"

"Yeah!" August beams, holding up the CD. "I rewatched the movie last week and I was like 'I gotta get this soundtrack."

"I swear no one's seen that movie! I love it!" Hathor smiles, bouncing on the balls of her feet. "Well obviously, 'cause it's campy *and* it has Rosario Dawson, like, come on."

"Yeah..." August agrees, deducing the extra layer in Hathor's praising. "And you've got... who's that?"

"Ida Maria!" Hathor replies, holding her CD up in turn. "She does like... rocky stuff, kinda punky, kinda personal... A friend recommended her stuff, and hey, they have it, so gotta grab a copy!"

"I love that! Who's the friend?" August asks, excited to hear more, especially about music.

"Oh... they're, like... an... online friend." Hathor admits, lowering her gaze and CD.

"That's cute!" August beams, leaning in a little, hoping to build Hathor up, never tear down. "Are you gonna meet up over the holidays?"

August's enthusiasm causing Hathor to perk up again, then deflate immediately at the question.

"Uh... well, we've never met..." Hathor elaborates, looking at her op-shop-bought, baby blue Vans, shuffling her feet. "Th-they live in W.A., so..."

"Oh, ok." August nods, invested and intrigued. "So, do you have any... in-person friends you're hanging out with?"

"Nah."

Swift. Clear. Teaming with deep loneliness.

"Well why don't you hang out with Celeste and me?" August suggests, absentmindedly picking at the plastic covering of the soundtrack she's yet to pay for. "We can all go on a friend-date!"

"Oh... are you sure?" Hathor asks, hoping that the answer will be 'yes'. "Wouldn't I be like a third wheel or something?"

"What? No!" August playfully pushes back, keen to make a new queer friend. "I'll make sure you're not a third wheel, if anything, I'll be the third wheel!"

"Maybe you and me will yammer on about music, and Celeste will be the third wheel!" Hathor jokes, before realising what she's said and hastily covering her mouth.

It's not quick enough, August hearing the joke loud and clear, throwing her head back in shocked laughter.

"You're funny!" She states, through chuckles. "Why didn't I know this before?"

"Probably because I usually mutter my jokes to myself." Hathor replies, giggling along. "That way, no one else can hear them."

"Ok, ok, this is gonna be fun." August says, putting her CD atop the scarlet Indie Rock 'M' card divider. "What's your number?"

"Oh... um... Ok, just don't say anything, ok?" Hathor requests, placing her CD down next to August's, and turning her fraying, grey backpack around, to pull out an ultramarine flip phone, with an obvious Telstra logo.

"What would I say?" August asks, genuine and confused, flipping her harlequin, cross-body handbag to the front. "It's just a phone."

"Yeah, but it's like... not an iPhone or Blackberry or whatever." Hathor rolls her eyes, showing this has clearly been leveraged against her before.

"And why would I care? I can still text you, right?" August asks, beaming and unbothered, pulling her Motorola Flipout from her cross-body handbag.

"Yeah! Yeah, of course." Hathor replies, flipping her phone open.

Hathor reading out her number, August entering it, pranking her, then both standing wordlessly for a moment, saving each other's numbers to contacts, the empty Stop 'N' Rock undisturbed for a brief few seconds.

Phones return to bags in silence, and it's August who breaks it.

"Ok! Well, I better go pay, I'm sure the person at the till thinks I'm stealing." She jokes, picking up the Josie And The Pussycats CD again.

"I wonder if that's because we're in high school or because we've got brown faces." Hathor whispers, low enough to not be heard by the reading clerk, turning the page in their copy of 'Things Seen' by Annie Ernaux.

It's August's turn to cover her mouth, turning immediately to Hathor, cackling behind her hand, hoping to not make too much of a scene.

"They're gonna think you're trying to take my pants off." Hathor whispers, smirking from ear to ear.

"Shut up!" August squeals from behind her hand. "Shut up, shut up, shut up."

"Ok, it's just-"

"Don't!" August protests, joyous tears forming.

"...just that, if you let me borrow-"

"Shut up!" August calls from behind her hand, knees squeezing together, trying to stay upright.

"...borrow that CD, you'll get the-"

"No, Hathor!" August jokingly objects, a free hand hanging onto the Indie Rock 'W' section for dear life.

"...the booklet back sopping wet-"

"Hathor!" August tries, doubling over completely.

"...because Rosario Dawson's on it."

"Oh my god!" August muffles, hand keeping most of the sound in, crumpled and gripping, absolutely losing it.

Hathor reaching out, monkey-gripping arms with August, delighting in being able to actually have fun with someone in real life.

Who knew, all this time, a friend was right under her nose, and now holding onto her for everything in this world.

Heavy breaths, steadying posture, and August is upright, shaking her head at Hathor.

"You're awful. I'm gonna text you tonight... about hanging out." August states, rummaging in her harlequin handbag, CD in the other hand. "Bring the good jokes."

"I'll go home and write up a bunch." Hathor playfully replies, giving a small wave as August heads up to the counter. "My team will whittle down to the real winners!"

August turns, shaking her arm playfully, trying to compose herself for the person bookmarking their reading at the till, and shooting Hathor some quick finger guns, before setting the soundtrack down on the counter, bank card in the other hand.

She busies herself, as she notes August paying in the corner of her eye, acting enthralled by the 'A' card of the Indie Rock section, hoping to not be weird and follow her new friend to the register.

Opting instead to wait for August to pay, wave goodbye, count to ten, and then go check out, like the Most Regular Human, just such a Normal Person.

So incredibly concerned with keeping this first meeting positive, and the least amount of awkward as possible. Nothing could be more important in this moment, on this day, in the Stop 'N' Rock.

1:19pm 2nd March 2011

I'm Here

To Eat My Own Hat

She's waiting for her moment, hoping to see a clear opening, an obvious sign that this might be a suitable time to swoop in. Though perhaps 'swooping in' isn't the best approach.

Regardless, she spots her chance.

August is putting away her lunchbox, getting out her water bottle, so this is probably the least-rude time to ask for her time, attention, and hopefully, her understanding.

Getting up from her spot, Hathor throws her fraying bag over her shoulder, and is suddenly feeling every cell in her body, as though she must be walking wrong, or swinging her arms too much, absolutely inundated with the overwhelming perception that she's somehow completely forgotten how to be a human.

She pushes it all down, trying against every impulse to just get over there, and say the thing, and then that'll be the thing done.

"A-August... can I... um, can I talk to you, please?" Hathor asks, standing a few good steps from August and a few others. "Um... alone?"

The Few Others look up with pure contempt, the most potent substance, delivered direct from the source: teenage girls.

But August closes her water bottle, and tucks it in her bag, looking up at Hathor with a plain expression, barely covering the deep loneliness.

"Yeah, of course." She agrees, standing and grabbing her brand new, pumpkin, backpack by the top handle. "Where's good?"

"Oh! Um, yeah… ok, l-let's go, um, over…" Hathor trails off, taken aback by August's openness, and suddenly without a go-to spot for this talk.

She signals to the science block, knowing it'll be quiet during lunch break.

August following in silence.

The walk only lasting a few seconds, but those seconds pulling out into agonising moments, compounding onto one another, discomfort stacking, a Jenga tower about to fall.

Hathor internally going over her dot points once last time, her lips moving silently as she's walking, staring at the concrete, noting the shadows getting so short, the walkway covering casting the entire path in shadow, dark grey and muted. A small respite from the beating, scorching, sun, as the Summer refuses to leave, digging it's fingers into the barren dirt, unable to be dragged away by the early days of Autumn.

It's just the blazing sun, the close footsteps of August, and the approaching science block, against the world.

Reaching the destination, Hathor just stops. Sudden and bizarre.

August pulling up as well, pausing for a couple of seconds, before asking:

"So, are you gonna sit down, or...?"

"Uh, yeah... yeah, let's sit down." Hathor replies, turning and crossing her legs to sit down, without thinking.

She thuds to the concrete, backpack dragging her down, dull pain ricocheting from her pelvis, up through her spine.

"Fuck! Are you ok?" August asks, dropping her bag and bobbing down. "Did you... hurt anything?"

"Yeah." Hathor replies, face contorted, trying to examine her palms. "But, can... we still talk?"

Thick laughter. Rushing through August's body. Absolute relief in this extremely strange situation. Trying to remain composed can come out in odd ways when push comes to Hathor-falling-on-her-arse.

Hathor joining in, the sting subsiding enough, as the chuckles fill her body, and she begins pulling gravel out of her palms, noting August sitting down with more grace and less bruised tailbone.

"You sure you're ok, but?" August asks again, wriggling around to adjust her position on the concrete, an attempt to tuck her bottle green school skirt under herself completely.

Hathor looking away, not wanting to be seen as trying to steal a glance as August adjusts. It's a bizarre averting, but no more awkward than anything else she's done in the last few minutes.

"Yeah, yeah I'm all good." Hathor affirms, meaning it.

For a brief pause, all is calm. No laughs, no footsteps, no bonking to the rock-solid cement.

"So…" August prompts, swinging her backpack around to sit on her shins, rummaging inside the pumpkin material.

"Yeah… yeah! Ok… so…" Hathor begins, recalibrating after none of this has so far gone anything like she practised, but somehow better than she'd feared. "The first thing is that I'm sorry. So fucking sorry, like… you tried to befriend me and I… with your girlfriend… and it was really not ok at all. And I… should have come to apologise sooner. That's also a part of it."

August takes in Hathor's words, hearing them completely, and in some ways, not wanting them, but knowing somewhere secret, that she needs them.

"Ok… thank you for that. Really." She replies, trying to force a smile, and failing abysmally, pulling a small packet of tissues from her backpack. "I guess I… don't really, like, blame you that much if I'm honest. I appreciate you apologising, like, I really do… but like…" August continues, fiddling with the tab on the tissue packet. "You weren't my girlfriend, you and I were only just becoming friends, we hung out twice, so like, honestly, I don't really feel that you owe me, like… clarity."

As the words leave her, she leaves herself. August drifting back to Celeste telling her of the dalliance with Hathor, to Celeste not telling her far more important things, to so many moments in which she can never be sure if Celeste felt even a flicker of what she felt for them.

Questions. All questions. And no answers.

At least not right now.

"Ok, yeah, I hear that." Hathor replies, dissipating August's thoughts with her calm and reassuring tone. "I still wanted to apologise, I think it's the right thing to do. You know, try and talk it out with you."

She considers August for a moment, wondering if this is the most miniscule shot in the deepest dark. But she'll never know, if she doesn't turn off the lights, and cock the gun.

"And... you can totally say no, but... do you think we could... like, you and me could... be friends?" Hathor asks, looking to August, who glances up from her tissue packet. "Like, work towards becoming friends, I mean."

August hears the words, but it takes a few beats for her to register them. To understand the request, the hope, the offer.

"I mean... I'm up for... working towards it. Yeah." She replies, a genuine smile coming to her now.

"Are you... is this a joke?" Hathor asks, barely believing it could've ever gone *this* well. "You mean it, but?"

"Yeah, I mean it." August asserts, as confused as Hathor. "Why wouldn't I mean it?"

"...because I like, slept with your girlfriend." Hathor replies, still waiting for the punchline, for the kick in the guts, for a bunch of people to jump out and yell at her for getting duped. "That's not always the best, like, place to start a friendship."

"Well, we can try." August shrugs. "I'm on the lookout for a new best friend, and like, no offence to those girls I was sitting with, but they're all straight."

"Really?"

"Not to quote Shrek, but 'really really'." August replies, devilish grin painted on her face.

"What the fuck?" Hathor laughs, bringing her palms to her face, before realising that's not the best idea. "Oh, shit!"

"That's what you get for disrespecting Shrek!" August jokes, head back and cackles boisterous.

"No, that's fair." Hathor relents, wincing as she takes a closer look at her palms.

August realising, halting her laughter in its tracks.

"Oh! Yeah, would you like one?" She asks, holding out the pocket tissues, having forgotten why she pulled them out a moment ago. "For your hands?"

Hathor pausing for a beat. Unable to fully trust such generosity and grace from someone she's so recently wronged.

But if she needs one thing: It's a friend.

And if she needs a second thing: It's a tissue.

"Is that ok?" She follows up, skittish and trepidatious in the face of such care.

"I wouldn't offer if it wasn't." August affirms, hand hanging in the chasm that is the innocuous concrete walkway.

The words coming to Hathor falsely. So foreign, despite comprehending every word. But the sentiment, the concept behind them, the intention and worldview they communicate, nothing could be more unknown.

But no time for processing, she doesn't want any pauses to be read as rudeness, not with a potential friendship on the line.

"Yeah, ok." She responds, willing the words to sink in. "Then... yes please."

"Should I...?" August asks, pointing to the packet. "Or do you want to?"

Hathor taking a beat to take the meaning in, then silently reaching for the tissues, with a small 'yeah, I can...' and a quick 'thanks' as she peels back the tab, taking one out, and handing the packet back.

"Should we go to the office?" August asks, pressing the sticky tab closed, and putting the tissues away.

"Nah, nah, it's not too bad, just like... grazes." Hathor explains, dabbing her palms. "I think it's more that I just slammed my face into them."

"Yeah, they don't look great." August agrees, trying to sneak a peek.

"Just a dickhead moment." Hathor half-jokes, trying to laugh this one off, like so many others.

"Hmm, seems like more of a forehead moment." August grins, continuing to try and peek.

"Did you fucking-?" Hathor looking up, such surprise and delight.

"No, you did." August jokes, dry and sarcastic, nodding with sincerity. "When you slammed your forehead into your fucked-up palms."

A pause. Thick as peanut butter.

And laughter. Roaring like a carnival. Refreshing like lemon. Restoring like time.

Reaching a fever pitch, winding down, petering out.

Silence creeping in, a dark figure in the doorway.

"But, seriously… do you wanna like, start the… talking about all this stuff?" Hathor asks, glad to have her scraped hand to return attention to.

"Maybe not… right now." August requests, knowing she doesn't have the space for it during her lunch break. "But I'm not like, harbouring hate in the meantime or anything." She clarifies, leaning in for emphasis, to conclude: "I mean that."

Hathor again finding herself in a land so unknown, as though August is a nation of her own making, with customs and language that don't rest on exhausting communication, and a debt of service for being born.

"Yeah." Hathor agrees, barely believing she got this lucky, and Celeste could ever get it so wrong. "Well, whenever you wanna talk it out-"

Her words drowned out by ringing. And end to talking and a resumption of classes.

"I mean, clearly now's no good." Hathor concludes, shrugging sarcastically.

"Nah, I think we can talk through English." August pushes back, brow furrowing ironically. "It's all about communication of ideas, so…"

"I'm sure Miss Fletcher would *love* that." Hathor jokes back, affirming and dry. "She's notoriously easy-going and not ever trying to belittle us."

"Just the actual sweetest!" August bursts, cackles escaping as she gets the words out.

Hathor joining in, students approaching, both trying to stand in their hysterics.

Awkward and joyous, bodies not co-operating, composure escaping the pair as others near. The inescapable web of being in on a bit, knowing someone else won't get it, weaving through the pair, thin and sticky, holding them to the cement, stretching seconds until they break.

All meaning one thing: these two are going to be ok.

10:09am 17th February 2012

ATARs And Accommodations

"Of course, Mrs. Zaki!" August calls, lying through her teeth.

"Ok!" Jamila returns, standing in the doorway, waving. "Call me when you get there, Pumpkin!"

"Absolutely!" Hathor replies, closing the boot of August's navy hatchback with a thud, and rounding the passenger side. "Wouldn't dream of forgetting!"

"Don't forget map! I put in glove compartment!" Rahim shouts, face against the fly screen, curtains pulled to his temple.

Hathor silently pulls it out, handing it to August, willing her to play along.

"Got them, Mr. Zaki! Thank you!" August calls back, holding them up and smiling. "Very kind of you!"

"Bye!" Hathor waves, sneakily gesturing for August to pull away. "Thank you both!"

"Bye, Pumpkin!" Jamila shouts, waving from the doorway.

"Yes, ok!" Rahim calls, dropping the curtains, disappearing from the window.

August doesn't need to be told twice, and puts the car into reverse, pulling out of what will no longer be

Hathor's driveway, and off down the suburban streets of Windradyne.

A loaded quiet flooding the hatchback quickly, meaningful and well-known by both occupants. Both feeling comfortable to allow it to build and swell, silent crescendo.

"Thanks for... you know, all that." Hathor mutters, breathing a heavy sigh.

"Yeah, of course. I'm happy to help." August replies, turning onto Suttor Street. "You saved me from starting at an empty Word doc anyway."

"I still can't wrap my head around you wanting to stay in Bathurst." Hathor responds, staring out the window, as the car passes the cemetery.

"I mean, I will leave. I'm just... not in a hurry." August responds, shrugging and unphased. "But I get why you would be."

"Mmm." Hathor hums, not feeling up to agreeing or disagreeing. "But, UNSW, here I come!"

"Yeah!" August agrees, deciding now is a good time to broch the subject she's been sitting for an hour. "I'm looking forward to the drive, by the way. I feel like we don't talk like we used to."

Hathor knows it's true.

In the wake of HSC exams, and the end of high school, their usual old faithfuls, of spending weekends sleeping over, days at the cinema, and nights driving around, have all become distant memories.

She'd marked it up to preparing for the move, excited to have her freedom. But in many ways, she was neglecting the person who helped her get through this final year.

"You're right." She agrees, watching the winding streets pass. "I'm sorry about like, ignoring you like that. It was shitty of me."

"I hear you. I guess I just... was hoping we could've spent more time together, before you left for uni." August explains, recalling the last three months, feeling somewhat like she was getting left behind. "That's why I was texting you so much."

"I know. I appreciate you trying to get in touch, and I'm sorry for being like, avoidant. It's just... I don't know, I had like tunnel vision or something." Hathor answers, turning to August, repentant. "It's like, all I could do... was think about getting to this point."

"Yeah, I hear that." August assures, grateful for this time. "I'm glad to be at this point."

"Well good, 'cause you've got like three hours of me." Hathor jokes, smiling deviantly. "Plus stops. We have to make stops to really stretch it out."

"Oh, I was just gonna move in with you." August volleys, sneaking a quick glance as she waits at the roundabout. "I assume that's ok."

"Yeah, I see no problem with that." Hathor throws back, comfortable and sarcastic.

"None whatsoever." August agrees, smiling.

"Not one at all." Hathor echoes, some of the humour falling behind as this reality sinks in. "I *am* really glad though. Like, genuinely."

"Yeah, me too." August nods, some of the intensity unnoticed by a usually perceptive soul.

"No, like, really actually." Hathor repeats. "I'm so glad to be out of that fucking house, and I'm so happy to be on the way to Sydney with you."

"Oh, thanks!" August beams, glancing quickly. "I appreciate that. I'm really happy too. I missed you these holidays."

"I missed you too." Hathor agrees, her last lonely months replaying, her evasion obvious in hindsight. "I was just... scared of missing you more, I think."

"That makes sense." August nods, taking in Hathor's words, eyes on the road. "I am an incredible friend, I don't know how these Sydney yuppies are gonna compare, honestly."

"They won't!" Hathor volleys, laughing heartily, relieved to feel so considered and much lighter.

"Alright then." August laughs along, a weight lifted in the sanctuary that is her navy hatchback.

Hathor watching the town she's known so well, and resented so intensely, fly by from the passenger side, freedom washing over her, a cleansing wave.

Anything is possible. This is the first day of her life. Not her mother's, not her father's, not even her sister's.

She can start living for herself, because she made it. She really made it through.

And a big part of that was August.

A compassionate, emotionally-intelligent friend, that her mother approved of, what more could a lonely, lesbian, Muslim, first-generation Aussie ask for?

Maybe a girlfriend.

But she has all of university for that. Three years of all new people, all new places, and far away from her parents.

She's coming up for air. And she's breathing deep. Her lungs filling like never before. Enough to ascend into the sky, and bathe in the clouds.

"It means a lot that you're the one driving me." She says simply. "It's like, you got me through my last year here, and you're taking me away too."

August smiling, clear from her profile, focus remaining on the road. Brown skin and dark curls lit by the relentless February sun, as it bounces around the untinted car windows, creating cascading colours. An angel on Earth.

"That's like a fairytale, I love it." She beams, glancing quickly, nose scrunching. "I'm like, oh! I'm your fairy godmother!"

"Well, I'll take you over my mother." Hathor jokes, half-meaning it. "She doesn't have any magic powers." She saves, worried her truth might come across as far too scathing.

"Not all of us are blessed with such power!" August volleys, noting the truth in Hathor's words, but knowing this defence too well by now. "And I'm all too happy to wave my wand at you." She adds, brandishing an index finger at Hathor.

Hathor giving a playful shimmy in response, bathing in imagined enchantments.

Pulling up at the lights, August looks over properly, hoping this drive will be as restorative as last year's April holidays, a chance to clear the air, and forge ahead, closer.

But she's no fool. She might not be able to keep this friend. So much is changing, and she can feel her teens slipping through her fingers, along with everything, and everyone, she's come to know.

She has the support of her parents, a part-time job at Maccas, time to pursue her writing, and fickle plans for travelling the world, once she saves up her own money. But who can say if any of her hopes will come to fruition, or how long any of them could take.

The lights change, and so does the subject, conversation moving on like her classmates, leaving town, going to university, starting jobs and apprenticeships, and she's spent the last three months staring at a blank page.

1:49pm, 18th January 2021

December and 2021

From: João-Mirella Jiménez
<j-m.jimenez@nastyknockout.com>
Sent: Monday, 18 January 2021 13:49
To: August Tandi-Andersen <augustta@live.com.au>
Subject: December and 2021

Hello August,
Happy new year!
I hope you're well and taking care of yourself.
You had great December sales, we're very happy with your promo for 25 Dec lead-up. Congratulations!
And it seems far way, but it's creeping up, so don't forget to do some socials promo for both your 2020 collection and "Under Neon Lights" in the lead up to 14 Feb.
Any thoughts, email or call!
You'll probably also get an email from Tiên today/tomorrow, everyone's back today, so you'll be getting any updates/replies this week.
Cheers,

João-Mirella Jiménez (she/he)
Marketing, Short Fiction and Poetry
Nasty Knockout Publishing Adelaide
Diverse Queer Stories From Diverse Queer Voices

Please consider the environment before printing this email

2:36pm 18th January 2021

RE: Re: 2021 Poem Collection

From: Tiên Phạm <t.pham@nastyknockout.com>
Sent: Monday, 18 January 2021 14:36
To: August Tandi-Andersen <augustta@live.com.au>
Subject: RE: Re: 2021 Poem Collection

Hi August,
Happy new year! A few key things:

1. Love the new batch. Changes working well. "A Memory For Cerulean Eyes" especially.
2. Nice filing off the serial numbers. We can't have a lawsuit from Breadseed Records.
3. We need 5-10 more, so keep 'em coming. I'll check in again in two weeks if I don't hear from you by then.

Talk soon,

Tiên Phạm (ze/zir)
Editor, Short Fiction and Poetry
Nasty Knockout Publishing Adelaide
Diverse Queer Stories From Diverse Queer Voices

Please consider the environment before printing this email

1:48pm 11th January 2021

A Memory For Cerulean Eyes

Memories are dangerous.

They hold one in a place.

A moment, a freeze frame.

They have no end and no beginning.

I don't want to be held in your memory.

Paused for all eternity, static-riddled.

My colours warped and my reality skewed.

I want you to learn about me as I grow and age.

Gaining wisdom and losing hair.

My body sagging and my beauty changing.

I want to meet you again and again.

Hear your new stories.

And listen to the revised versions of the old ones.

Don't hold me in your memory.

Hold me in your arms.

Dear Reader

Thank you for purchasing, and reading, '*Under A Summer Sky In January*', and, as before, if you're skipping to the end, please go back and read it first. I promise you can come back to this letter once you've finished the story.

But we can never read a story for the first time again, so savour the unknown, and read it unspoiled while you can.

So, you've finished the story of August, Hathor, and Celeste. Three layered, flawed, and beautiful characters, all of whom I love very much.

I hope you enjoyed their journeys, felt their pains, and maybe even saw yourself in their missteps, their lived experience, or attempts to make amends.

This was a difficult one, I'm not going to sugar-coat it. I thought setting a story in the town I went to high school would mean it'd be easier to add local details, and help it feel grounded.

But it brought up a lot of old emotions, but I hope I've sewed them into the story well.

As before, I wrote a love story without a traditional Happily Ever After, and a somewhat unconventional narrative structure.

Hopefully, you enjoyed both the human bittersweetness, and the head-spinning feeling of jumping around the story's timeline, like adults recalling their teen years.

Thank you for reading, and inviting my words into your life. I appreciate it very much.

Kind regards,

Neptune Henriksen

About The Author

Neptune Henriksen is a critically acclaimed writer and theatre maker, as well as an award-winning director.

Their works explore identity, sexuality, and emotional turmoil through a queer, intersectional lens, with love, humour, and introspection.

Their art is prolific and varied, from storytelling to comedy directing, microfiction to physical theatre, with their artistic voice always shining through, unique and clear.

Their works seek to comfort, to explore, and to shed light on topics often shied away from.

Other Works By The Author

Queer Summer Trilogy, 2022-2023

Three novellas of queer romance in the Australian Summer.

1. *'Where The Pink Meets The Blue'*, a bisexual erotica – available Dec 2022

2. *'Under A Summer Sky In January'*, a sapphic teen love triangle – available Jan 2023

3. *'We Used To Hold Hands All The Time'*, A romance of childhood friends reunited – available Feb 2023

'Daydreamings: A Collection Of Connections', 2020

A flash fiction collection, snapshots of moments of connection and relationships of all intersections.